BREAKING EVIL

Ensouled: Book Two

KRISTINA RIENZI

Book Layout: Kate Tilton (www.katetilton.com)

Cover Design: Kari March Designs (www.KariMarch.com)

Editor: C.S. Lakin (www.livewritethrive.com)

Proofreader: Christie Stratos, Proof Positive (www.proofpositivepro.com)

Author Photograph: Jaime Lynn Photography (www.JaimeLynnPhotography.com)

Indigo Hawk Group
Shrewsbury, New Jersey

For the men in my life: my husband and my father. Without your love, I wouldn't have written a single word in 2015, or ever again.

CHAPTER 1

PRESENT DAY

Athunderous boom sent tremors throughout the rustic mansion. Sera jerked upright, wide awake. She had been sharply startled out of a deep sleep, dreaming of simpler times when she was still human.

A cacophony of voices lingered in the distance. Sera stilled to listen more carefully.

"What exploded in our house?"

It sounded like a bomb had gone off in their foyer. Or at the very least an earthquake had hit, unlikely for New Jersey, but not impossible. The deafening roar had awakened Damon.

"I'm about to find out."

Damon shot up as if he was prepared to not only defend his property but also their lives. Residual trembling persisted as if it was, in fact, the aftershock of an earthquake. The continual shaking was inside of Sera's bones, too.

Sera arched her back to stretch. Her neck spasmed violently. Instantly, she froze, allowing her muscles to relax. They had extended to their tearing point and snapped back into place like a rubber band. Desperate for relief, she massaged the back of her neck and shoulder.

Damon was already out of bed and clearly on an unstoppable mission. Sera watched as he moved without hesitation, on high alert and not wasting a second. He flung open his closet doors and skimmed the contents, then threw on a thermal shirt and a pair of jeans faster than Sera had ever seen before.

Sera briefly met his gaze, trying to slow him down so he would wait for her. It was no use. The digital alarm beamed in red. Four in the morning. Way too early to be up. Still groggy but with her nerves on edge, Sera swung her legs out of the bed until her feet hit the floor.

She had become a supernatural badass over the last year. She wouldn't allow any battle to be fought by Damon alone. Her elite status wouldn't be wasted. Especially when it came to protecting the man she loved. And their home.

Once out of bed, Sera joined Damon at the door. "Ready?"

"Where do you think you're going?"

The veins in Damon's neck bulged. His demeanor told Sera he was unwavering in his resolve. The man was equipped to grant any invader their death wish. Without any help.

"With you. Where else?"

"Like hell you are."

"Exactly. Like hell, I am."

Damon lunged into the hallway without her. He turned and looked back sternly. "Stay put."

He slammed their bedroom door behind him. Damon's behavior stunned Sera. They were supposed to be a team. Team members didn't leave each other alone and helpless. Especially not when there was a threat.

Was she supposed to wait until she was attacked in their bedroom? Sera stomped her foot hard.

"I'm not some damsel in distress. I'm a demon, damn it.""

She acted like a teenager and didn't care. The adrenaline made her want to kick ass something fierce. She fisted her hands and pumped them at her sides.

Even if Damon had heard her, he wouldn't have changed his mind. Before she was done complaining, Damon was already on the main floor. It sounded like a first-class ruckus. She could hear him thrashing around as he moved from room to room. His search and attack mission was akin to a tornado ripping through the house. Any angry demon was a force to be reckoned with, especially when that demon was Damon. His soft exterior gave no clues to the real wickedness inside of him. He was as evil and ruthless as they came, and she loved him for all of it.

There was a resounding whoosh of their giant front door being swung open. Damon had gone outside. Sera slid on her robe in a hurry and hightailed it to the window, taking a look.

Sera had long ago proven she would fight to the death; a truth she had prided herself on. But Damon was adamant. Sera had no choice but to acquiesce to his wishes. It wasn't about being an obedient girlfriend. It was about being smart. And not getting herself killed.

Damon had a tremendous amount of experience in the world of the supernatural. Far more than Sera. She wasn't going to start learning how to survive by unnecessary trial and error in her new world unless it was forced upon her. He had been the one to teach her everything she needed to know up until that point. She had to trust him this time, too. Damon hadn't always been straightforward with her. However, his deceptions had always been for her sake. And for her survival.

One thing was for certain, Sera trusted Damon with her life. He would protect her no matter the cost to him. Even if saving her meant he would ultimately lose her. He had proven his loyalty to her time and time again. In turn, she respected him for his unique demon qualities, even if she didn't always agree with how he chose to express them.

In a rush, Sera parted the curtains and peered outside. She couldn't see a thing. The ceiling fixture shone too brightly in the bedroom creating a terrible glare, blinding her. Realizing the issue, Sera sped to the other side of the room to flip the light off. In her path, appearing seemingly out of nowhere was a sneaker. It tripped her. She tried hard to catch herself on the dresser. As she did, a horrible memory flashed in her mind.

Her father, lifeless in his bedroom after his fatal fall.

There was no way to stop her fall either. Sera hit the hardwood floor with a substantial crash. She shrieked aloud, more out of frustration than from the pain. Annoyed and groaning, she pulled herself upright using the side of the bed for leverage. When standing, she flicked the light switch off in the room. Finally, it was as dark inside her room as was needed. She cautiously walked back to the window.

She got a better view of the street this time. It was more than dark outside, as the clouds covered the moon. From what she could see of the sky, it looked battered and bruised, with blue-black swirls mixed with shades of the deepest gray. The sun wasn't ready to rise. No light was present to illuminate their private cul-de-sac. The seclusion of their home was something she had always loved about the old place. As well as its aristocratic feel, one mixed with a mild sense of doom. It conveyed a warning for anyone who might consider coming into the neighborhood in the evening looking for trouble. The mystic ambiance of their surroundings offered them some additional discretion and protection.

Not that they needed it, but it calmed their minds. It allowed them to relax more than most demons who were often anticipating a fight at a moment's notice.

The entire neighborhood seemed to lie comfortably

under a thick blanket of darkness. Sera leaned closer to the glass, cupping her hands around her face to focus on the area directly in front of her home.

The fog was thick, hovering close to the ground. Although she couldn't make out many details, she was able to see something peeking out of the dense dew. Immediately, she wished she hadn't.

The scene on her front lawn below made no sense. She shook her head in confusion. Was she hallucinating? Perhaps she was still dreaming. Her neck muscle pain and throbbing hip told her she was wide awake.

Reality was becoming a nightmare.

An army of demon hunters lined her yard in a V-formation. They looked more like a billiards set-up than a murderous gang. There had to be at least twenty-five of them. Dressed head to toe in black military fatigues. Their silhouettes became more and more visible as the dense fog drifted away. Assembled and prepared for battle exactly as they had been years ago when they had fought in New Jersey.

A front line of hunters, who were to be barriers protecting the pool balls behind them—more hunters. The line was dressed in their own version of fire suits. These suits made their bodies bulge all over. They resembled little kids decked out in below-zero snow gear. Only the hunters in this fire gear were armed with weapons.

Their armaments were efficiently deadly. With a mere press of a button, every edge of the wearer's clothing would burst into flames. They could take out any demon in a ten-foot radius in an instant. The media had made sure to thoroughly propagandize these effective fiery-wearable weapons to the point that when demons caught sight of these special suits, it sent them into a panic.

As if the fire suits were not enough, each hunter had strapped around their body what looked like an M-16 fully automatic rifle. Demon hunters never carried the same type of assault weapons that humans used in ordinary undertakings, such as shooting targets and/or intruders.

Traditional bullets slowed a demon down but didn't kill them. Instead, the hunters had developed a newly improvised firearm. They used a powerful gun and filled the shells with a highly explosive substance instead of gunpowder that would burst into flames upon impact. These firearms were guaranteed demon killers.

The fireballs, as they were dubbed, were nearly impossible to purchase because they had been declared illegal. Only a select few had access to this demon-killing ammunition in case of an all-out war. It was apparent demon hunters were preparing for a world war on a daily basis.

Demon hunters were not a civil group of law-abiding citizens. They were criminals who called themselves vigilantes. As criminals, they, too, found a way to get their hands on the worst kind of illegal contraband. They weren't rule followers who cared about right, wrong, and the consequences. They paid no mind to the laws. Therefore, the laws were not a deterrent.

Sera's gut clenched. The hunters had come for them. Damon didn't stand a chance against their enemy. Everything happened so incredibly fast that she hardly had time to digest it all. She was completely vulnerable for the first time in her demon life as she watched, unable to intervene, while a large group of demon hunters dragged Damon off of their front porch.

The sound that had awakened her must have been the hunters charging the front door. When Damon had opened the door, they must have immediately grabbed him.

The hunters mercilessly pummeled him to the ground. Sera cringed as she watched the man she loved being forcefully taken from their home. Within a split second, he was gone.

Those sadistic killers had kidnapped him, without warning, into the early morning darkness.

"No!" The word burst out of Sera like a deep guttural scream, one full of fury and anguish. It was primal and terrifying.

Her heart fell, pained beyond recognition, and her knees buckled in response. She braced herself to remain standing. The old physiological-emotional reactions carried over from her human days impacted her now. She feared collapse.

Out of the corner of her eye, she saw the vibrant diamonds from her wings on fire pendant shining brightly. The stones caught the light and sparkled, igniting something more powerful within her. Rage surfaced like never before, manifesting into a living piece of her soul. She embraced her rage as it grew stronger, fueling the fire coursing through her veins and summoning her fierce demon within.

Her entire body flexed and straightened with the force of her demonic power surfacing. She was re-energized, renewed with heated strength and readiness for battle. There was no stopping her now. She was willing to take it as far as she had to. Murdering everyone and anyone who crossed her path on the way to save Damon was not too much. Her body had transformed with pure anger. She had no pain at all, only a furious desire to rip those hunters to shreds.

With Damon as their captive, Sera was the next logical victim. Quickly, she scanned their bedroom for any hidden intruders. She refused to get caught off guard, so she checked everywhere. Sera threw herself on the floor until she was flat on her stomach and wiggled her way under their enormous custom-made king sized bed. Confident the bedroom was safe, fury still rushed through her system. She feverishly changed into clothes she could fight in.

Time was of the essence. Sera burst out of her room and into the hallway and raced down the long corridor. As she reached the winding stairs, she opened her mouth to scream that she was coming for Damon. But before she could say anything, a booming crack silenced her. It bellowed loudly.

The noise stopped her in her tracks. She had no idea where the sound had come from. Dazed, she froze in her steps and looked around, trying to identify its source. Her blood pumped fast through her system. When she took her next step, an excruciating and undeniable agony came over her. She had been attacked.

Stars swirled and danced in her vision. Everything dimmed. The back of her head throbbed. The pain pounded in her skull, making a *ba-boom* sound over and over again. Without further warning, her body gave way, and she dropped fast to the hard floor. As she fell and desperately tried to right herself, she spun on the perfect angle to see the reason for her unfortunate circumstance. He loomed over her, poised for a further assault.

Her attacker was a dark, blurry figure. He watched her collapse with his small beady eyes glaring at her from the holes in his black mask. While the hunter's face was obscured, his smile gleamed brightly in the dimly lit house. Sera could have sworn she heard laughter. It was a note higher than she anticipated. She noticed the hunter's right arm; he was positioned ready to strike. He wielded a giant baseball bat, which had just connected with her head.

"What the...?" Sera's rage metamorphosed into energy, thrusting through her like a roaring and violent storm. It readied her body to respond to her attacker.

The hunter pulled his arm back slowly until it was raised high above his head. He paused, a cocky move, meant to intimidate her.

Unwilling to fall victim to the masked assailant, Sera

summoned her supernatural strength once again and pushed herself off the floor to face him. In a flash, he twisted his body and swung the bat toward her. Sera hesitated a beat too long, just enough for the demon hunter to get his wish.

She had been mere inches away from an upright stance when the bat, in full swing, connected with her cheekbone. The impact sent Sera careening backward until she slammed up against a wall.

For seconds she teetered on the edge of the top stair. Finally, she lost her battle with her balance and slid off the wall. To save herself, she took a leap high into the air. Nonetheless, her body tumbled and crashed down the steps of the grand staircase.

The fall felt as if it lasted for minutes, but only seconds had passed. Conscious as she experienced her soar through the air, her body twisted and turned as it made its way to the bottom of the stairs. Without warning, her head smashed violently onto the marble foyer entrance. Everything faded to black.

CHAPTER 2

C J stared at the dead cell phone for a beat before tossing it on the counter. She didn't care if it smashed into tiny pieces. Intense irritation sprouted like an unrelenting weed, threatening to take her over entirely. The frantic search for an appropriate or inappropriate release of her pent-up anger had begun. Relief needed to be found. Soon. An explosion of epic emotional proportions was imminent. And deadly.

"Tomorrow? I can't wait until tomorrow. I need to do something *now*. No. Right this second."

Sweat poured from the CJ's brow. On a battle high from the night before, she paced around the kitchen in mad circles. Around and around. Dizzy but unable to stop. Her hardened heart raced with full force. A complete conversation brewed inside of her shattered mind, only half of it spoken aloud to the empty room.

"Action. I need to take action. He wants me to wait? Ha! Of course he does. But I can't wait. There's no time. Not a minute to waste. Why is he making me hold on?"

She shook in disbelief.

"I didn't want this to happen. I tried to stop it. But I have no choice now. I must take action. Action. All I can do is take action."

CJ was going crazy. About to spin out of control. A crash against the window forced her back to reality.

"Damned birds."

She grabbed a short glass, threw in a few ice cubes, and searched the refrigerator. Transitioning to day drinking over the course of the last year had been easy. Traumatic events metamorphosed a person, changing them entirely until they became a shattered version of their old self.

CJ needed to calm the distorted thoughts. Dull the horrific memories of demons, the ones making it difficult to concentrate and impossible to breathe. Modern life was one giant horror show starring sacrificial demon hunters and malevolent supernatural beings. Walking around pretending everyone was rational and kind was no more. No kindness was left in the world. None at all.

Slumped over her tablet at the kitchen table, her makeshift office, she began editing the drafted email.

Date: Thursday, September 4, 2015
Time: 7:30 a.m.
Subject: URGENT
In T-minus seventy (70) hours, our yearlong plans, the war we've all been training for, will finally begin. You're officially on call from here on out.
I'll be in touch when I get orders from my insider tomorrow afternoon. Until then, your safest bet is to focus on preparing your militias. Stock up on all forms of ammunition. Most importantly, go forth and behave normally in your life. Don't draw any suspicion. No one—not even your dogs—can know what we're about to do.
Godspeed, my friends.

CJ

Once the email went through cyberspace, CJ's breaths came a little faster. She bubbled with excitement for what was about to take place. The pieces were falling together now. Every evil bastard would finally get their punishment of an eternity in Hell.

CJ stared at the cross ring. She spun it around on the middle finger a demon had sprained a year ago. The finger had healed. The suffering remained.

A hard knock drew her attention to the back door. *Another bird?* CJ stretched up on tiptoes to see who was there. A demon. She cracked the door open.

"You're nuts. It's daytime. What if someone sees you?"

"They'll think I'm checking up on Lorenzo's hired help."

The burly demon pushed into the house. CJ backed out of his way, almost tripping and closed the door and the blinds.

"Are you?"

"Sure. That's why I'm here. Go ahead. Show me what you've got for the big day."

"Not much has changed since last week."

The demon pushed up against CJ, chest bumping the hunter. "Show me anyway."

"Right this way."

"For old time's sake."

Clearly, he had more than one agenda for his visit. He knew where she was taking him. But he played along, as he always did. The demon trailed an inch too close behind her.

"Get off my back."

"Not a chance...in Hell." The demon laughed vigorously.

When CJ got to the landing and turned down the hall, the door of the annihilation room was already cracked open. The demon shot CJ a devious look.

"I told you to keep that room locked."

"I can only take orders from one supernatural being at a time."

CJ thrust the door to the annihilation room open. "Here's the latest."

The demon's eyes grew wide. "Shit."

"I told you. Not much has changed."

"Except for the walls. You sick..."

"Watch it. It's called strategically driven motivation. With examples."

"I'll say."

The demon carefully examined the newly installed floor to ceiling wallpaper on the far side of the room. A DIY version made from old newspaper clippings, photographs, and other anti-demon memorabilia. CJ stood tall and smiled, proud of the artwork. Like a mural, every inch of the one wall was covered. The rest of the room still needed to be decorated and would be in time. The masterpiece before them told the horrible story of the life CJ lived not so long ago. The one that drove the demon hunter leader to emerge with a vengeance. While her artistic tribute hadn't done any justice to the pain brewing inside of her—and never would—it provided a historical record and the justification for her new path in life.

The demon pulled up close to a particular cluster of photographs. Most of the pictures had been taken directly from newspapers and magazine clippings around town. With no shortage of propaganda, supplies were easy to find. Local Jersey Shore residents were as tough as spikes. CJ was no different. When it came time to address the rumors of a potential demon war, they stocked up on plenty of weaponry. They had no intention of losing any upcoming battles.

For the center wall ornamentation, CJ selected a few

grotesque images printed straight off banned websites. One in particular drew the demon's attention. He rubbed the symbol of the branded wings on fire on his left shoulder as he examined the images. Her favorite photograph, the same one making him uncomfortable, was a group of rogue demons who had been captured by hunters. They had regularly waited outside of the biker bar, Hell's Bells. That particular weekend night they had gotten lucky. The group of rogue demons was wasted. Their minds didn't work well enough to use their supernatural powers. Hunters had taken advantage, forcing them with fire into the back of a van where they were imprisoned in cages.

The photographs depicted demons undergoing torture moments before they were set on fire and killed. All of this had happened on Barnacle Bay, the beach at the end of the Maroon County peninsula.

The demon moved closer to the wall. He pointed to the red dots splattered all over his people. CJ was afraid the pictures might have been too much for him to handle. Too late now. He pointed to the red dots.

"Is that...?"

"Blood." CJ had no reason to lie.

"Not..."

"My blood." CJ pulled up her thin tee shirt, baring a six-pack still healing after being recently sliced apart.

"Serious anger issues, huh?"

"You can't blame me."

She nodded at the main attraction. A picture of Sera leaving work at her father's firm, Enzo and Dell. CJ had drawn a pair of horns and a devil's tail on the demon leader's daughter. The demon gave CJ a side-glance and an accompanying crooked smile.

"Whose side do you think I'm on?"

CJ waved the demon out of the room. "Enough of this depressing end of world bullshit. I have something I want to show you."

"No, you've got it all wrong." He kicked the door open. "I'm the one who has something to show you."

He threw CJ across the room and onto her bed. Only their heaving breaths broke the silence as Alex pinned CJ on the mattress. He brushed his lips lightly over hers and stopped. She reached desperately for him, but he pulled away. He did it again, and again until she couldn't take it anymore.

CJ growled. "Alex, c'mon. You know I hate when you do this to me."

"You love it. You've always loved it."

CJ moaned beneath him. He was right. She did love it. Within a few seconds, she fell quickly into submission from his familiar touch.

"You're the master. Go ahead. Unleash your darkness all over me. Lord knows I've got my own to unleash right back."

"No one, not even your Lord, can help you now."

Alex kissed her hard. Her mind went blank. She was completely numb. She forgot all about what, not who, she was in love with. Pretending and wishing he were human wouldn't make him so, but it helped put reality out of her mind.

What started as a soft exchange turned passionately violent as the couple tumbled off the bed and onto the floor, landing hard. CJ and Alex never stopped ripping at each other. The need inside of them both was insatiable. The long-standing passion deep beneath the surface had finally been released after months of idle flirting and innuendos. She didn't care if he was everything she hated. CJ had darkness within her too, and it begged to be released. He was her release.

They shared darkness one no one else would ever understand. When this human and demon merged, their sinister desires followed. They swam blindly in the evil between them, ignoring what the world told them they needed to be, right up until they drowned in each other's embrace.

CHAPTER 3

Sera peeled her eyelids open one at a time. Unforgiving fluorescent overhead lights seared into her eyes. She shifted slightly. Pain surged through her body. A grumble escaped her. She looked around the room for evidence of what had happened. Her entire body throbbed and pulsated. She hadn't known she could feel anything so intensely. Someone had surely set every single one of her nerve endings ablaze.

Dazed and without clear vision, she was relieved to see Damon's handsome and compassionate face hovering over her.

"What the hell happened to me? Where am I?" Her voice cracked unexpectedly. *Have I lost my voice, too?* She swallowed hard and tried to clear her throat.

"You're in Demon General." Damon caressed her hand.

Bits and pieces of memories flooded back to her as a dream sequence, filling Sera's mind. Black hooded figures were taking Damon away. She coughed.

"You're okay? I was coming for you. I didn't make it. Someone..."

He gently pushed a lock of hair away from her face. It calmed her.

"Demon hunters attacked you after they took me."

"Hunters let us live?"

Damon looked off into the distance as if recalling the whole nightmare.

"They held me in a pit surrounded by fire. I don't understand it all myself. I shouldn't be here right now. I shouldn't be alive."

"Hunters never release their victims until they're a pile of ash."

All that had happened to them was uncharacteristic of demon hunters. It made no sense. Damon examined his reflection in the glass, seeming to consider Sera's words.

"The only thing that matters is that we both survived."

Horror raced through Sera. She imagined the scene Damon must have come upon when he got back to the house.

"How'd I get here? Did you find me?"

"I wish. I didn't get to you in time. Hunters dumped me in the center of Main Street in Red Reef. By the time I made it to the office and tried to find Lorenzo, Gina told me he'd already found you and brought you to the hospital."

"Word travels fast, huh?"

"To Lorenzo it does. One of our neighbors called the police. Amato got involved."

It was all he needed to say. Amato had worked with Damon for several years when he was a detective in the local police department. Even as a human, Amato had always admired Damon and they became fast friends. A kinship existed between them that couldn't be explained. They understood each other. Amato ended up becoming the insider Lorenzo often used, even more so now that Damon worked for Lorenzo directly.

Sera searched her mind for details of what happened right

before she blacked out, but it hurt for her to think. The heartbeat in her injured cheek pulsated wildly.

"How long have I been here?"

"A couple of hours, maybe."

"That's all?" She massaged her face gently.

"Leave it alone. It will get better."

"Easy for you to say. You didn't break your face."

"Give yourself a chance to heal."

Sera rolled her eyes. They'd had their share of trust issues in the past, but it was all behind them now.

"I wish you were a vampire so your blood could heal me."

"You with the vampire references. What? A demon boyfriend isn't good enough?"

Sera tried to smirk, but her face ached too much.

"Don't make me laugh."

"Careful."

What a joke. Sera was far from careful, risking her life day in and day out. She did what needed to be done. Not what was safe. She shifted into a comfortable partially seated position.

"So, tell me...wise one. If they were demon hunters, why aren't we a pile of ashes?"

"Good question. Hunters don't know the meaning of mercy. Who else could it be? There's no new enemy. The same demon-hating humans have been after us ever since we stepped foot on their planet."

"Lately it seems like hunters are everywhere. I bet Lorenzo's happy about that."

"Furious is more like it."

"Fury is his happiness. I'm sure he's thrilled to have a public and purposeful reason to go after demon hunters. Scratch that—humans overall. Especially since they've attacked his daughter, all bets must be off."

A nurse walked in, interrupting them. Her opal eyes shimmered in the luminous hospital lighting like rare brilliant cut diamonds. She pointed to the whiteboard. Her name was scribbled in black marker.

"Hi, Sera. I'm Maxine, the RN in charge of you during your stay at Demon General."

In charge of me? "Hi."

"How are you feeling?" Maxine examined Sera's face. The nurse's gaze drifted down Sera's body, inspecting her from head to toe.

"What time can I get out of here today? I have plans tonight I can't miss."

"Of course. I understand."

"Lorenzo won't expect you to show up for dinner in your condition."

Sera shot him a pointed look. "I expect me to show up for dinner. I'm not going to let a couple of bumps stop me from living my life."

"Concentrate on getting better, love."

"When will I be released?"

"You need to heal some first," Maxine said.

"There's no time for me to recover. I need to go home."

She pulled the covers aside to prepare to get out of the bed. Maxine rushed to Sera's side and tucked her back in.

"Soon enough, Sera."

"If you won't make it happen, I'll have to release myself."

"Not necessary. We're in the process of getting authorization from your father for your medication. Then we'll have you on your way shortly."

Sera whipped her head in Maxine's direction. "My father?"

"No need to get upset."

"My real dad is dead."

"I apologize. I meant Lorenzo."

"I needed an insurance company to authorize everything when I was human. Now the demon doctor won't provide the appropriate care for me until Lorenzo approves it. You'd think being the daughter of the ruler of all demons would make my life easier. At the very least, healthcare should be at the top of the list of core benefits. Instead, I'm still jumping through hoops and at the mercy of someone else to decide if I'm worthy enough to be one of the healthy ones."

"A little pretentious, are we?" Damon joked.

Sera shot him a dirty look. "I'm not in the mood to laugh."

"I promise it won't be long. Until then, would you like something to eat?"

"It's not like I have anything better to do."

"Be patient." Damon grinned.

"You're quite the comedian over there with your healthy head and intact face."

Maxine waved to the woman waiting in the hallway with a tray of food. She entered the room and placed the food on the table beside Sera's bed and swung it around in front of her.

"Thank you, Carla." Maxine shooed the woman away.

Carla flashed Sera a look of disgust. If Carla was the one in a hospital bed, she wouldn't have received half of the treatment Sera had. It was a shame the way things worked with the privileged getting all of the advantages in life while everyone else suffered. Maxine pressed a few buttons on the side of Sera's bed, moving it into an upright position.

"Your meds are on their way."

"Yup," Sera said.

Maxine pulled the curtain closed and shuffled away. Damon lightly kissed Sera's broken cheek.

"Told you. The doctor will discharge you in no time. Like I said."

Sera flashed a fake smile in between her spoonfuls of chocolate pudding.

"As long as they let me out of here, I don't care what they're giving me. Prescription drugs, street drugs or some supernatural invention...whatever...I'm game."

Sera took a swig of her juice. A few minutes later, the curtain slid open again. A doctor with a sly grin waltzed into her room. He held a tiny plastic cup in his hand. Sera gave Damon a strange look. Typically the attending physician didn't administer the medication himself. An abnormal course of action in a human hospital. She wasn't going to question the demon hospital administration process.

"I'm Doctor Winston. We don't take your injuries lightly here at Demon General. You endured a brutal beating. Not to mention, as I understand it, you have important plans this evening."

Dr. Winston walked closer, handing her the medication. Sera took the cup from him. She peered inside of it. A clear liquid stared back at her. She attempted to swirl it around. The thick substance, akin to cough syrup, barely moved. She lifted it to her nose and took a whiff. Surprisingly, it had no scent at all.

"What is this?"

"Blaze. The best thing to ever happen to you."

She looked to Damon for recognition. He shrugged. Neither of them had ever heard of it.

"Is it an experimental drug?" Not that she should care, but she was curious.

Dr. Winston's smile was a beat off, although she had no reason not to trust him. "I prefer to call it medicinal innovation myself."

Sera considered declining it, but she was in awful shape and had nothing to lose.

"Go for it," Damon said.

"Bottoms up." She downed the medication and handed the cup back to Dr. Winston.

"Good girl."

Almost instantly, an emotional and physical relief washed over her. All at once and all encompassing. She wasn't sure how it was possible, but the pain evaporated into thin air. She had no desire to complain.

"Sit back and relax while you heal."

Sera closed her eyes as she fell back. Using her handheld remote, she lowered the bed. Getting lost in the effects of her medication was the only goal. The bump on the back of her head minimized in record time. The throbbing in her cheek dissipated. Soon she couldn't feel anything at all. Her entire body fused back together into perfect shape. In no time, she was a brand new woman.

"Blaze is a miracle cure."

"Sure is. We save the best for the best." Dr. Winston smiled.

It didn't seem fair, but she had no right to argue over a medical miracle she didn't understand. She was thankful to be feeling better. And so quickly. In fact, she felt better than she had ever felt in all of her lives. A few moments later, Sera shot up in her bed, energized.

"When can I leave?"

"Your discharge papers are already complete. Feel free to go whenever you're ready. Good day."

Dr. Winston pulled the papers from his folder and laid them on her tray table. He promptly exited the room. As Sera flipped the pages, she noticed a tiny, ragged piece of loose-leaf paper peeking out from the middle of the bundle. Curious, she made sure Damon wasn't looking. Pushing the table away, she turned on her side as if positioning herself to get out of bed. She pulled out the note and quickly unfolded it. The words on the tiny piece of paper immediately made her nauseous.

Beware of the truth.

For a brief moment, Sera considered sharing it with Damon. He was the one person in the world she loved and trusted. She decided against it. *At least for now.* Instead, she folded the note and shoved it in her underwear, the only storage place on her person, which was currently in nothing more than a thin hospital gown.

Her heart pounded hard in her chest. Sera took a deep breath and threw her legs over the side of the bed. A part of her swarmed with guilt for not sharing the note with Damon. She felt as if she had betrayed or cheated on him. No secrets were ever kept from Damon. Her supernatural experience taught her it was better to ask for forgiveness rather than to get permission this time.

Her thoughts raced. *It's happening again. Do they know my secret?* Damon must have noticed she was trying to stand up. He rushed to assist her.

"Hang on."

Sera pointed to the counter where she saw her bag. "Can you hand me my clothes? I want to get out of here."

Damon started to walk over to get Sera's belongings when the ultimate bearer of negative energy waltzed into her hospital room.

"Not so fast."

CHAPTER 4

L orenzo sauntered over to Sera. He was calm and relaxed, as always. He sat on the edge of the hospital bed next to his daughter.

"You, my dear, look like someone who's gotten a new lease on life. Am I right, or am I right?"

"I'm recovering. You should know. You're the one who approved my secret cure. What was that all about anyway?"

Damon shifted, obviously uncomfortable. "I'm going to grab some coffee."

Lorenzo ignored Sera's question, responding to Damon instead. "Good idea."

"I'll leave you two alone," Damon said before leaving the room.

Lorenzo rushed Damon off with an annoyed expression. He turned his attention back to his daughter.

"I know who did this to you."

"It wouldn't take a genius to figure it out."

"They say we're evil. Nonsense! Humans are the truly evil species. They're the torturers. The murderers. Even worse... the cowards."

"You're on a mission to kill every single human being because any one of them could be a demon hunter, aren't you?"

Lorenzo walked slowly over to the window and peered out at the morning sky.

"Your mother loved to watch the sunrise. I'd take Rafaela to the beach every Sunday morning. Her bright smile was infectious, radiant beyond measure. Even more so than the sun itself. My rotten heart skipped a few beats back then."

"I didn't know that," Sera said.

"She was the only person to ever make me question what I was and what I wanted from this life."

Everything he said was true, even though he hadn't remembered how it felt to love anyone. The raw emotion had been artificially summoned for Sera's benefit now. He caught sight of his daughter out of his peripheral vision. Her expression fell hard at the mention of her mother. An emotional reaction he had desperately wanted to evoke. He held back his smile.

"What do demon hunters have to do with my mother?"

Lorenzo turned his attention back to the rising sun as he spoke. "They're the reason she died."

"You're wrong. Alison killed her. She told me herself."

Alison, Sera's former demon best friend, had confessed to killing Sera's mother, her biological father, and her demon psychiatrist and family friend, Vera. Lorenzo hadn't liked Alison. He had only tolerated her because he had needed to use her to further his agenda.

"That's what Alison wanted you to believe. But that's because she was psychotic."

"So she didn't kill my mother?"

"Alison did what she said she did. She showed your mother a version of your future that Rafaela dreaded. I'm sure a part of it killed her that day. But Alison isn't the one who influenced my dear, sweet Rafaela to take her own life. Alison couldn't have done such a thing, even if she wanted to."

"Why not? Alison was a demon. My mother was human. It seems pretty self-explanatory."

"So long as your mother was wearing the angel pendant I gave to her, no demon could ever harm her. In fact, no demon could make her do anything at all."

Sera blinked hard, grabbing the diamond wings on fire hanging around her own neck, a gift from Lorenzo as well.

"Angel pendant?"

"The same angel pendant your father gave to you for your sixteenth birthday. It had belonged to your mother once. Of course, I hadn't expected him to tell you the truth about it. In my opinion, it's a detail you should have always known. It might have saved you some stress in the last few months of your human life."

Lorenzo knew Alison had stalked and targeted Sera, who not only threatened his daughter's life at every turn but also kidnapped her best friend, Jenna. While Sera hadn't known it was Alison at the time, Lorenzo wished Sera had benefited from feeling protected by the angel pendant she had always worn. While not as powerful as the wings on fire pendant he had given her—the one she had in her possession today as an Ensoul—the angel necklace would have eased her mind back then.

"I had no idea it had any power."

"Wearing it meant no demon could have taken your life. Or controlled you. Two things that were, and still are, paramount to me."

Sadly, Lorenzo had allowed her to believe the angel pendant was a gift from the man she thought was her biological father, Michael, as a beautiful memory of her mother. Lorenzo knew she regarded the angel pendant as a symbol of her guardian angel mother watching over her. She couldn't have been more wrong.

"And the demon hunters?"

"They went after your mother because of Alison. She convinced them all that Rafaela was pure evil for giving birth to you. Since Rafaela was human, she was an easy target. Of course, Alison had a gift for playing both sides to perfection. At the time, I had no idea she was conspiring against me."

"I can't see anyone being so stupid."

Sera raised her eyebrows at Lorenzo, seemingly astonished at his bravado. Lorenzo looked away, feeling the loss all over again and all at once.

"Taking Rafaela away from me was a direct attack. But I needed Alison as an ally nonetheless. So, yes, I used her in many ways, as she strategically used others. Yet I never forgave her for the part she played in your mother's death."

"I guess that explains your hatred for humans."

Lorenzo had carried good intentions on the earth once. But losing Rafaela changed everything back then. Having Sera as an Ensoul changed it once more. He choked back the emotions caught in his throat, ones he hadn't expressed in two decades.

"I had no choice. They slaughtered Rafaela."

"They killed my mom."

"Demon hunters—humans—took Rafaela, your mother and my only love, away."

"Murderers," Sera said.

His words came out in a throaty growl filled with hate. "I've never forgiven them."

Lorenzo knew Sera understood his loss. She had expressed her terrible grief when her parents died, even if for different reasons. He knew she wouldn't blame him for the way he felt about humans. Sera wasn't a hypocrite. Soon enough, she would understand and come to his side, acknowledging his malicious intentions were just.

"Now they're after me." Sera shifted uncomfortably.

"That was expected. What I hadn't anticipated was the breadth and depth of their master plan."

"What master plan?"

"You, my dear Sera, are only one piece of the convoluted puzzle that will impact every supernatural being in existence."

"How do you know this wasn't a single attack?"

Lorenzo walked closer to Sera, helping her stand even though she didn't need any assistance. The Blaze elixir he ordered her to take had worked its magic. In fact, she looked perfectly healthy in all ways.

"You do realize your brutal beating was more than an attack? A strong message like that is one I must respond to, and as soon as possible."

Damon walked in raising both of his hands in the air. Noticeably, he was not holding a coffee cup. He cracked a smile.

"Would you believe the industrial machine was broken? I went to a few of the other floors, but none of the break rooms had a pot of coffee that wasn't burnt to a crisp. I should have known. Demons aren't exactly java experts."

"Perfect timing. I'm ready to go. This place is making me sick." Lorenzo stepped closer to Damon.

Sera's gaze darted between the two most important men in her life. "But..."

Lorenzo placed his hand on Damon's shoulder. "Take care of my girl. She's going to be better than fine, but rest will do her good. Tonight's going to be a big night."

LORENZO HEADED TO THE DOOR. HE GLANCED BACK AS HE strolled out of the hospital room. *I hope she shares my little story with Damon. Too bad it's a total lie.*

Halfway to the lobby, his cell phone started to ring. He answered the call he couldn't miss. "Well done."

The shaky voice on the other end replied, "Thank you for the opportunity. It was exhilarating! When's my next assignment? I'm hungry. I need to keep moving or—"

"Don't get too excited. You'll never be allowed that level of access to my world again."

"But you said—"

"I said I'd give you demons. And I will. But they will be at my discretion. Understood?"

A long, uneasy sigh sounded in Lorenzo's ear. "I do." The caller paused. "But will you tell me when...where? I need to prepare for the next attack. It's not as though this is easy for me."

The caller's feet were stomping on an unforgiving floor.

"From the looks of your end result, I don't believe you for one second. You're lucky I didn't take action against you for doing your job too well."

"Oh, I..."

"It's fine. I never expected perfection. You're human."

"Any idea when you'll need me again?"

"Soon enough. Have patience. I have bigger plans for the both of us."

"What plans? I need to do something. Right now."

Lorenzo pressed the unlock button on his key fob. It chirped as he walked swiftly to his turbo-boosted race car.

"Listen to me. You're in a high-ranking position, albeit on the other side. You need to calm down. Drink a glass of wine. Take a pill. Do whatever you pathetic humans do to get yourselves under control. I can't have you acting like a completely insane narcissist. This isn't about *you*. Focus on the bigger picture. And cool it."

"You're right." Her voice was a high-pitched signal of her anxiety.

"Excellent."

"But I need a plan. I can't idly sit around. I have to do something. Anything. You understand, don't you? After all that's happened to me, you must understand my desperation to act."

"I do. Remember, we need each other." Lorenzo paused.

"We do."

"I have a plan, one which I intended to execute much further down the line. But time is of the essence now. Tomorrow afternoon you'll get a phone call with detailed instructions. Follow the orders exactly. Don't ask any more questions. It will all make sense when you arrive."

"I'm ready. In fact, if you'd like, I can be ready tomorrow morning or tonight even. Do you want me to take action tonight?" Her voice rose with each word.

"You're not listening to me. I said tomorrow." Lorenzo gritted his teeth. "Get a grip on yourself. Don't push your luck or you'll regret it."

Lorenzo hung up. *Overanxious demon hunters are almost as much trouble as rogue demons.* The thought gave him an idea. He slid into the leather seat of his high-end sports car and revved the engine. It roared to life. He backed out carefully and sped out of Demon General's parking lot like the devil himself was on his tail.

He pressed on his satellite radio to the hair band station playing metal and rock tunes from the eighties. Lorenzo turned the volume up until he couldn't hear himself think. He lowered the windows. The wind rushed through his hair.

He was headed straight for Hells Bells, the local rogue demon biker hangout. The last place on earth Lorenzo was welcome. The anticipation of the looks on everyone's faces when he walked in made him smile and his heart beat faster for the first time in a long while. He cackled like a warlock as he flew down the highway.

I can hardly wait to see you all burn and rot in Hell, you bastard traitors.

CHAPTER 5

JUNE 1, 1993

Vera's story distracted Rafaela. She scanned the mall-goers looking for a face in the crowd. She didn't know whom the face belonged to, but the rumbling in her gut told her she would find out soon enough.

"Tell me more." Rafaela tried to sound interested, but the feeling wouldn't let her go.

"Not much more to tell." Vera looked away. "I wish I could have helped him, but it was time to cut ties."

"Sounds like you did the right thing."

The guy seemed like a psycho if Rafaela was being honest with herself. She supposed most of Vera's clients would sound that way. Vera stopped to feel the fabric on a dress for sale.

"Treating his mental health issues was one thing," Vera said. "But when I became his distraction, I ceased to serve his best interest. It was time to end our professional relationship."

"You're not afraid he'll come after you?"

Rafaela realized the stupidity of her statement. Vera was a demon, albeit one with a heart. She was well equipped to handle herself if needed.

"I'll cross that bridge."

The women turned down the mall corridor toward the coffee shop. A remarkable man seemed to appear out of nowhere and began walking beside Vera. He was impossible to ignore. The pit in Rafaela's gut waned. She knew precisely why. The man leaned into Vera as if he were listening in on their conversation. Rafaela didn't understand why Vera didn't see him. Or she did see him but ignored him. He was obviously hitting on Vera.

Rafaela needed to say something without being too obvious. She elbowed Vera lightly, hoping she would turn to her side and see the man. She disregarded Rafaela and kept talking. Frustrated beyond belief, Rafaela stopped dead in her tracks. It took Vera a few steps to realize what her friend had done. She doubled back.

"Did we miss a sale?" Vera asked.

The man followed close behind Vera, smiling at Rafaela. Her heart thumped hard.

"Behind you," Rafaela finally said.

When Vera turned around, her face paled for the briefest of moments. "You scared me half to death."

While an odd statement for a demon to make, Rafaela knew Vera would have preferred being human. Still, Rafaela had no idea how such a gorgeous man could scare anyone. Let alone Vera.

"That's what I do best, my dear." The man winked at Rafaela. The energy he emitted blinded her. She couldn't see straight. It was electric.

Vera rolled her eyes. "Rafaela, this is Lorenzo. Lorenzo, meet my best friend, Rafaela."

When Rafaela had first seen him, she thought he might be interested in Vera. Not anymore. The way Lorenzo devoured Rafaela with his eyes told her one thing and one thing only.

Lorenzo lifted Rafaela's hand. He kissed it in an old-fashioned, romantic hello, one she might have snapped her hand back from if it hadn't been attached to the striking man before her.

"It's an honor to meet you, Rafaela."

His gaze never left her. It was as if he was trying to mesmerize her with his eyes. Mesmerize her he did.

"Same here."

Rafaela couldn't think straight, nor take her eyes off the wings on fire tattoo on his forearm. It was the sexiest tattoo, and placement, she had ever seen. Even more so because he didn't cover it up like Vera did with hers. Soon, the twosome became a threesome. Only now, Lorenzo was walking beside Rafaela instead of Vera.

It took only a few minutes for Rafaela to become so engrossed in conversation with Lorenzo that it was as if Vera wasn't even there. Lorenzo's dark brown eyes, almost black, drew her inside of him. She was transfixed, as if in a trance, although it was completely natural to her to feel this way with Lorenzo. She supposed most women felt that way. Lorenzo had the *it* factor. So much so that Rafaela hadn't noticed when Vera left the two of them alone. She must have said goodbye, but Rafaela couldn't be sure. What she was sure of was that her best friend would forgive her for rudely ignoring her departure. The stunning and charming man had been a distraction she didn't mind.

Before going their separate ways, Lorenzo and Rafaela exchanged phone numbers. She decided she wasn't going to call him. This time, she refused to chase a man who gave her sparks, especially not a man like Lorenzo. This time, Rafaela wanted to be the one who was pursued. This time, she wanted it to be real.

CHAPTER 6

PRESENT DAY

Lorenzo raised his champagne flute. "To Sera. You're the change I'm ready to see in the world. Our new supernatural world."

The other guests mimicked Lorenzo's gesture. "To Sera."

Sera graciously nodded at the compliment. Everyone clinked their glasses together and sipped on their perfect, overpriced bubbly. The extravagant, lavish party was held in a private dining room at the newest five-star restaurant in Red Reef. There were no limits to Lorenzo's riches or Sera's gratefulness for his generosity. Damon massaged her hand under the table. He placed a gentle kiss upon her lips. Sera's cheeks warmed. She was not used to the increased attention her new position brought. She would rather have been plotting her takeover of the world behind office doors than celebrating anything so publicly. Nevertheless, she accepted the support, smiling brightly, and raising her glass to Lorenzo in thanks.

"You're gorgeous," Damon said.

His lips moved in admiration. She longed to kiss them once again. Instead, she gazed into Damon's opalescent eyes, recalling when she barely knew the man behind them. Sera's heart fluttered. A day never passed when she didn't stare at the man beside her in pure astonishment. All he had done for her, all he had risked day in and day out was more than any woman could ever want.

"Is that how I landed such a hot boyfriend?"

"Tonight's all about you."

"I couldn't have come this far without you."

Lorenzo stood, taking ownership of the dinner table. He had something important to say. Everyone took notice and hushed.

"Our plan, as you are all well aware, is to make life better for humanity. The world is in dire straits these days. Humans killing humans. Brothers and sisters turning against each other. Demons would never consider such self-deprecating acts."

Lorenzo's guests guffawed aloud at the state of humanity and disgusting human behavior.

"Terrible," a demon yelled out.

Lorenzo dropped his head in shame. "I never thought I'd be saying this, but since Sera became one of us, the bloodshed has escalated. Demon hunters are on the rise, evidenced by the attack on my dear daughter. Honestly, I don't think we have another moment to waste. Do you agree?"

The room hooted and hollered, yelling affirmations like, "Hell, yes!" and "Let's do this!"

Sera whispered to Damon, "I feel like we're at a tailgate party instead of a formal dinner. What's going on?"

"Ah, this is typical Lorenzo hyping up his regime. Whatever his next steps are, he wants his people ready at a moment's notice."

"What do you think he wants us to do now?"

Damon looked at her and raised his eyebrows. "I believe you know the answer."

"Go to war?" Sera shook her head. "I can't accept that.

We're not prepared for a total takeover. I should say, I'm not prepared." She took a gulp of her champagne to calm her nerves.

"Well," Damon said, "get ready. Because based on the scene here tonight, it won't be long before it's executed."

Lorenzo's voice boomed over the cheers. "In a few short hours, we'll put our long-awaited plan into action. I'll be giving you assignments first thing in the morning. Be prepped and primed for anything and everything, my dearest friends and followers. This is what we have trained for, ever since we learned that the real definition of equal rights in the eyes of humans is persecution."

He pointed to the crowd, with his commanding personality spilling from his very pores.

One of the dinner guests shouted, "You're the savior humans have been waiting for all of this time." The rest of the crowd yelled in support.

"Savior?" Sera couldn't believe her ears.

Damon shook his head, looking as embarrassed as Sera at the spectacle everyone was making of themselves.

Lorenzo puffed out his chest and grinned broadly. "I'm pleased you understand the role I'll play in our new world. And as extensions of me, each of you is a savior in your own right. Not only to save humans from themselves, but also to save your own race. The demon race."

More shouts of affirmation resounded.

"Quiet, quiet down now." Lorenzo raised his hands to control the high-spirited crowd. "I have one more announcement to make."

The room was silenced. Sera and Damon shared a curious glance.

Lorenzo's eyes scanned the crowd, finally landing on Sera. "Sera, my darling daughter. Would you please stand up so everyone can see you?"

Sera cautiously stood and glanced around the room.

"There she is. Won't you come up here with me?" Lorenzo beamed at her, and the room grew loud with applause.

"I hate attention."

"Just go."

Damon gave her the nudge she needed. When she reached the front of the room, Lorenzo greeted her with a hug. The coldness of his touch wasn't something she would ever get used to, even as a demon.

"As I mentioned, it's time for us to take serious action as a demon race. But I can't do this alone. Nor would I want to attempt such a feat. For us to be successful in our takeover of humankind, we need to have healthy, well-developed and powerful demon leaders paving the way."

The takeover of humankind. The words swam in Sera's head, making her stomach swirl with uneasiness.

"That's why you're here tonight. You'll be a leader in what I'm coining the New World Regime. Each of you will have your own team following your every order, which will come from me." Lorenzo paused for a moment. "And Sera."

He grabbed her hand. The snakelike texture of his palm made her quiver.

"That's right. Sera will be my second in command, taking the position of Director of Special Demon Forces, choosing one other demon as her partner. I'm sure we all know who it will be."

All eyes turned to Damon, and he waited for his cue from Sera on how to respond.

Special Demon Forces?

She raised her eyebrows at Damon. Sera expected to be named a high-ranking leader in Lorenzo's regime at some point but assumed it would be after she had gotten comfortable with being supernatural. She also had never anticipated being his second in command. According to her estimations, she expected to become a level above the other demons in the room, as one of his loyal senior leaders. Her newest promotion of second in command, essentially a vice president in leadership, would bring a tremendous amount of pressure, none of which she was ready for. Especially since she disagreed wholly with his plans.

Sera smiled to all in the room and nodded to Damon. The crowd burst into cheers.

Lorenzo raised their joined hands, lifting them into the air as he proclaimed his enthusiastic joyfulness.

"To the New World Regime!"

Sera's glance darted across the room and out the window. Her focus landed on a woman standing outside. She was dressed all in black. Her long ginger hair fell down over most of her face. With her one uncovered eye, she stared directly at Sera, then disappeared into the night.

AFTER THE MEAL ENDED AND THE DINNER GUESTS WENT ON their way, Damon and Serafina moved to the bar to join their fearless leader for cocktails. Lorenzo's eyes brightened when he saw Sera. He pulled her close in a tight embrace. His actions reminded her of the photograph Vera showed her when she learned he was her biological father. He had the same possessive embrace with her mother.

Beware of the truth echoed in Sera's mind.

"My darling daughter, we've come so far, haven't we?"

"We have."

Sera disagreed. She had never felt like his daughter, only his employee, which she supposed was more than when they first met. Besides a few logistical items like her job, residence and, well, the physical changes, everything else in her supernatural life seemed to be the same as when she was human.

Of course, her best friend, Jenna wasn't by her side any longer, but she was confident she would change her mind about Sera over time. At least Sera hoped Jenna would.

"And we haven't even touched upon your abilities, which is of the utmost importance now." Lorenzo sipped on his top-shelf whiskey.

"That should be fun."

Sera wasn't ready for any abilities. To her, pretending in her mind that she was still human worked just fine. She had hoped for a little more time to enjoy her safe state of super-natural denial. In fact, being supernatural hadn't been what Sera expected at all. To date, she hadn't experienced anything she couldn't handle. Oddly enough, her human life had thrown her for more of a loop than anything she had experienced as an Ensoul.

"I think it's time. Don't you?"

Lorenzo winked at Damon, his gorgeous white teeth glistened in the bar's lighting. He squeezed Sera closer as if to say, *she belongs to me first Damon, and don't you ever forget it*. She cringed at his touch. Damon raised an eyebrow, playing along.

"Absolutely." He turned to face Sera. "You're long overdue for a splash of supernatural excitement in your life. What better time than now, when we're preparing for..."

Lorenzo cleared his throat. "Yes, training will be perfect."

Sera swung her head around and shot Damon a private look so he would stop egging Lorenzo on. Even though they were both well aware whatever Lorenzo wanted, Lorenzo got. If he said she needed training now, it was a matter of mere days, maybe even hours until he forced it to happen.

Sweat began to trickle down her neck. Suppressing powers she didn't understand would prove to be tremendously difficult. Sera's shoulders fell in surrender. She casually took a sip of her drink.

"When do we start?"

"When you least expect it." Lorenzo hadn't hesitated in his answer.

"Guerrilla style?" As a fake laugh came from her, a shiver crawled up and down her spine.

"We'll begin with basic training in my office."

"Gee, I was looking forward to hitting up the gun range or boxing ring at the very least. I am Director of Special Demon Forces, after all, right?" Sera was half joking and half serious. She hoped to experience actual combat training if she was going into the fight of her life.

"Not needed, my dear." Lorenzo released his grip on her. "Your power isn't behind the barrel of a revolver or a pair of boxer's gloves."

Sera's darkest fear was opening her mind, her most vulnerable place. She hated acknowledging that the longer she lived alongside Lorenzo, the less she wanted to betray him. Obviously she had a lot to think about. It wasn't going to get resolved in one night, certainly not after five glasses of a top-shelf champagne. Once more, she would leave it up to fate as to how it would all play out, which is precisely how she had handled her entire supernatural existence.

Sera smiled in forced adoration at the man with narcissism embedded in his dark soul. "I can hardly wait."

"Excellent. That's exactly what I expected you to say." Lorenzo picked up his snifter glass, and in one fell swoop, he drank it down. He shook off the effects of the amber liquid.

"Another drink?" Damon asked.

"Not tonight. My time is up. I'll see you both soon. Remember, don't let your guard down."

A loud chuckle escaped Lorenzo as he headed for the door. Right before he exited, he stopped and turned his head toward Sera. He regarded her in a way that made her genuinely uneasy. Unnaturally dark eyes with shadows hovering beneath their surfaces stalked her. His glance gave her chills.

Sera quickly put the image of him and her unsettling feelings out of her mind. She snapped back to her bubbly self, and her bubbly drink. Damon nudged her shoulder as if to say, don't let him get to you. She tossed back her drink and ordered another.

"I was thinking..."

"You think?" Damon smirked.

The light-hearted interactions between them put her at ease.

"We may have the wrong plan in mind."

Damon's face tightened and his brows furrowed. "Our plan is not wrong."

"Up until last night, things had been so quiet since I transformed. I'm not convinced that destroying humankind is still Lorenzo's master plan. What's the harm in following his lead? Why can't we leave things as they are for a while?"

Damon's back straightened. He slammed his drink down hard on the bar.

"You didn't die so we could do nothing. Deep down inside, I don't believe you want us to sit back and assume Lorenzo has good intentions after what he said. Our takeover of humankind can only result in destruction for everyone involved. That can't be what you want."

Damon shook his head vigorously, his disapproval evident. He clearly wasn't ready to entertain her logic, especially after everything Lorenzo had done.

"Lorenzo has killed people. Humans have died by his hands and the hands of his followers for no good reason. Don't you think I know that? I realize he believes he is just in his actions, and I can understand his way of thinking, but I still can't agree that innocent humans should die for what others did in the past."

"You agree with me, then?"

"No, I don't agree at all. Since my transformation, Lorenzo has behaved himself. He's contained his evil expertly as far as I can tell. I haven't heard of anything he's done wrong; everyone said he used to brag about his vicious acts all of the time. As for his detailed plans to take over humankind, I believe he wants to make life better for all of us. Look at what the demon hunters are doing. They got us, Damon. Two people who are at the top of the demon hierarchy. Lorenzo started out with good intentions, didn't he? He can't be that far off now."

"First of all, the hunters didn't get us. They threatened us, which is entirely different. They sent us a strong message. Nothing more. We would be ashes if they did what they really wanted to do to us the other night. As for Lorenzo, you're right. He began his journey on Earth with amiable goals. At least that's the persona he showed the world back when he agreed to be a proponent of peace. But things have changed. Drastically."

"I'm not sure if he's been deceiving me to gain my trust or if he has changed and maybe it's because of me. I could be the reason why he's motivated to put a plan into action. Maybe, just maybe, my near-death experience terrified him, and the part of him harboring feelings, the part tucked away in the pits of his soul, was worried he might lose me."

Damon rolled his eyes. "It has nothing to do with you, Sera. Lorenzo doesn't have the capability for worry, nor for love."

"Either way, I'm having a hard time maintaining a plot to betray the man who not only gave me the privileged life I have today but gave me life period."

Damon ran his fingers through his hair, clearly frustrated. "He's showing you what he wants you to see, as he always does. It's how he operates. You know this, yet you're still taken in by his devious methods?"

Sera looked down and away. She tried to convince him and maybe herself.

"He's been good to us, Damon. I don't see how we can turn our backs on him."

"Our plan isn't about us living a good life. It's about your people, human beings, merely having a life left to live."

"I know what you're saying. You're right. But if I use my powers against the one person who gave them to me in the first place, I'll be nothing more than a traitor. Besides, being so close to Lorenzo over the past year has given me a new perspective."

"You won't be a traitor. You will be brave. Life has never changed for the oppressed by others sitting around ignoring the problem or wishing it away. Life has changed, it has gotten better because someone extraordinary stood up and fought for it. That someone needs to be you. You see what you want to see right now, what's comfortable for you to see. I don't blame you at all. You've been to the depths of Hell and back in human terms. I can understand you want a break from the craziness. But I promise you, the devil inside of Lorenzo will come out. For the sake of humankind, I hope you see his devil sooner rather than later."

Sera understood his conviction. Humans weren't oppressed. Life moved along just fine. Until it didn't, Sera refused to be the one to shake things up. The pot needed to stir on its own.

"You said it best. I need to see it for myself."

CHAPTER 7

L orenzo had a taste for murder as he strolled along the polished sidewalk of Red Reef. He adjusted his suit jacket, straightened his back, and arrogantly looked around. Then he spit on the ground proclaiming his disgust for the world. Foolish humans. They had no concept of what it meant to be alive. They didn't appreciate the oxygen they breathed into their lungs, nor the sun on their skin. If they did, it would prove they valued something more than the money in their bank accounts. Humans took their physical lives for granted on every level.

Lorenzo had taken it upon himself to continually teach humans a lesson. They never seemed to comprehend it. They never learned from their mistakes either. His strategies hadn't worked. That's why it was time for a new plan.

He summoned his driver, Yohan Martin, curbside. He was all business when it came to Lorenzo. A Haitian immigrant who hoped to find a piece of the American Dream, Yohan had found the ruler of all demons instead. Lorenzo had forgone driving his exotic sports car. He had no intention of going home that night. His mental acumen, not unlike Sera's endurance, needed a challenge. Unlike humans, his financial focus was a means to a greater end. Not a status symbol. Maybe he wanted it to be a tad bit of a status symbol. Still, he had worked for it. Lives had been lost. His place in the financial hierarchy—and world—had been earned. It was rightfully his. And his alone.

Yohan drove Lorenzo around Red Reef for a few minutes. He had enough of the boring goings-on in his community. The window dividing the passenger area from the driver rolled down.

"Where to this evening, sir?"

Lorenzo rarely admired humans, but when he found Yohan peddling on a street corner in Alcove Park, Lorenzo couldn't resist. There was an admirable darkness within Yohan that drew Lorenzo to him, inch by devilish inch. With the right amount of money and persuasion, Yohan would keep his mouth shut and do whatever Lorenzo wanted him to do, even when the human wasn't under any of his supernatural influence. It was a daunting task for demons, even an Ensoul like Lorenzo, to keep humans under control for long periods of time. Lorenzo was ready for an easier life. Yohan had found the American Dream after all.

Lorenzo barked at his driver. "Alcove Park."

Yohan quickly closed the window between them for privacy. Still, for fun, Lorenzo had made it a habit of planting horrific ideas in Yohan's mind and then sending him on his way. The bloodshed that ensued was minimal compared to what Lorenzo would have done. He found a rewarding and sadistic pleasure in having his own human puppet.

Lorenzo fingered the vial on the inside of his jacket pocket. *I am the Puppet Master.* He laughed to himself. No human being was exempt from becoming his puppet in the end. It would happen much sooner than anyone could have dreamed. For now, all Lorenzo wanted to do was to put his mind, and the back of his limo, to proper use. Luckily, he didn't have to venture far at all. It was only a handful of miles until they reached Yohan's old stomping grounds. The easiest place for a demon to have an enjoyable time.

Lorenzo watched the world go by outside of his tinted window. Revulsion was the only feeling he carried for humanity. Humans had nerve blaming demons for the evil in the world. They were the wrong ones. Their senseless murders of their own people. The travesties they allowed to go on. Yet they could never see it. They would never look in the mirror and see the maleficence living in their souls. Instead, they blamed the natural target: demons. And so Lorenzo would ensure their blame would be well placed.

He pulled the small vial out of his pocket and admired it. He held it up to the moonlight. "You'll change the world. Yes, you will, my little friend. You'll blaze through all of us."

The limousine shook as Yohan hit a pothole. Lorenzo was careful not to lose his grip. He had more than a substantial supply to hold the entire population of the planet over, but he preferred to use it wisely.

When Yohan slowed to a speed below the posted twenty-five mile limit, Lorenzo was alerted they were close without having to look. His cue to ingest the entire vial in one shot.

The warmth of the elixir he named Blaze for its ability to surpass all supernatural dreams, putting fire to shame, made him quiver. It was exhilarating. A sense of power and strength flushed him. Everything seemed to brighten. The endless stars in the night sky sparkled like rare diamonds. The world opened up to him. It was all for his taking. His heart galloped. His muscles pulsated with the markers of a man on a mission.

Only this man was supernatural and more powerful than any human could ever imagine.

Lorenzo had been operating under the influence of Blaze to condition his body and brain for a time, soon to come, when supernatural beings would no longer be pressured to conform. No more hiding behind a three-piece suit. It had taken a while, but Lorenzo had learned to control himself. Except for when, by choice, he didn't.

He pressed the intercom from the back of the stretch limousine. "We're here."

Except for the town name, Lorenzo never told Yohan the address of where he wanted to be taken. The driver was instructed to drive around until Lorenzo's intercom cue advised him when he decided they had arrived at their destination. Yohan pulled the car over on a dimly lit, pothole-riddled block. Most of the old Victorian-style houses were dilapidated, abandoned and or condemned, except for one in particular. The one Lorenzo had been watching and saving for a rainy day—or night.

As he almost never did, right before opening the door, Lorenzo changed his mind. "Move on."

About five or six streets away he would begin the night-marish evening. He instructed Yohan to go to the place where brothers sold their sisters and mothers sold their daughters. Although no funds would change hands tonight. By the time Yohan had parked, the residents of the drug-infested neighborhood were practically lined up and ready. Money attracted attention in Alcove Park. Nothing said financial independence better than a stretch limousine.

Lorenzo exited the symbol of wealth his onlookers would never experience in their lives. He scanned the crowd. About fifteen adults and twenty-five children stood before him, begging and pleading for a handout. They offered him everything, precisely as he had expected, handing over their wives and children for only a few dollars. He laughed at the irony. Part of him almost walked away, knowing what he was about to do was more of a service to humanity than an injustice. That was no fun for Lorenzo. But he needed them to warm up to the main event.

He closed his eyes and simply thought about the crowd falling under his control. All forty-plus of them obliged. One by one the children walked away, wandering home without their parents. Their fate would be their own tonight. In the spirit of Sera, he had decided to give the little ones a fighting chance. *Just this once.* The adults, on the other hand, had no such luck. Those weak excuses for human beings piled into his limousine until they were hip to hip, both on the seats and on the floor. When Lorenzo got in behind them, he slammed the door and locked it.

As Yohan slowly cruised the streets, all of Lorenzo's humans seemed pleased to be there. They all sat calmly, oblivious to the mild trance Lorenzo had put them in, right before everything was about to change. He took the other vile of Blaze—the one he had made into a spray bottle as a matter of convenience—out of his other pocket. While the potency was diluted tremendously—one-part Blaze elixir to one hundred parts water—it was more than enough to turn them into his puppets.

To ensure his experiment was a success, he had engineered the next few moments perfectly. First, Lorenzo released the humans from his mind control spell. Chaos ensued when the passengers realized a supernatural madman had kidnapped them, albeit a wealthy one. With seconds before the situation got out of control, he sprang into action. Lorenzo sprayed his unique formula into the air. He turned up the fan, ensuring every one of them breathed it in. The more frustrated and panicked they got, the faster it was ingested. The better it was for Lorenzo.

Before long, all of the humans were in a trance. Some were even drooling. Had he used too much? *Nah!* The formula would need to be perfected for the next time, sure, but this version would do for now. He marveled at his puppets, knowing they were an example of the future all of humankind.

The zombie effect eventually wore off. He waited it out patiently. As each person regained his or her awareness of reality, the true Lorenzo emerged. He showed them no mercy. Some of them slashed their own throats with a box cutter while others gouged out their eyes. All the while they were awake, alive and dying a painfully slow death.

Each time when Lorenzo was done slaughtering a body, he would go on to dismember it with his own hands. Limb by limb, he took the former human apart, throwing each body part into a pile in the middle of the over-stretched limousine floor. Then came the real fun.

As one after another awakened, he or she would tremble in horror, realizing what Lorenzo was about to do to them. To make matters worse for them, Lorenzo ensured they saw him in a state all humans feared: sharp teeth; long, pointed nails; two horns on his head. Humans hallucinated the devil with natural ease. He appeared the way they wanted to see him, the way they needed to see him to believe his actions fit his persona. No man as handsome as Lorenzo could commit such horrendous acts. Humans too often used appearance alone to judge. What they failed to see was the devil living inside of every human being, not only the one living within the demons.

After Lorenzo had disposed of the first round of bodies, he instructed Yohan to continue the routine. He drove a few blocks, and he picked up more victims, and on and on. As the count rose, so did the stench. They made a final trip to an abandoned park where he burned the remains in a massive bonfire. On their way back home, Yohan made a pit stop at the house they had pulled over in front of earlier in the evening.

Lorenzo's appearance was now bloodied and ghoulish. He exited his car and straightened his suit jacket. Without hesitation, he strutted to the front door and rang the doorbell. Inside, he saw his handpicked family of five watching television. The outside porch light was broken so when the woman of the house came to the door, she was unable to see Lorenzo clearly. It didn't matter, because when the time came, she didn't have a moment to react, not even a second to scream.

Lorenzo pushed the door open in a wild frenzy. He attacked her first, and then ripped apart each member of her family one by one. They watched his brutal violence come to life as he mutilated each person. No coercion was needed. The sheer force and speed with which he worked left them unable to defend themselves. No battle took place. No resistance given at all. It was over in mere moments.

Lorenzo had no vendetta. No score to settle. He didn't even know them. He had seen the parents with their kids in the park one day as he passed through town. It had struck him how happy they seemed with their simple human lives. How the sheer pleasure of them being together had brought them joy. Lorenzo hated them for their happiness because it was a lie. In his world, joy didn't exist.

Only evil.

After he had finished his bloody mission for the evening, he paused to evaluate his handy work. He smiled in satisfaction at their formerly quaint home, which was now a macabre horror scene.

Lorenzo was more than a demon. More than evil. He was a devil. In truth, it was what all beings were, but only the demons had the courage to take responsibility for their evil.

Lorenzo's job as the leader of the demons was to bring them to their full potential.

He left the house and got back into the limo. He hit the intercom button.

"To my estate."

CHAPTER 8

After leaving the bar, Sera and Damon strolled arm in arm through Red Reef. At one point she caught him in her peripheral view and thought, *Damn, I'm a lucky woman.* She couldn't help but admire his striking profile. His sharp features and soft heart made her swoon, something she had never allowed herself to do when she was human.

Sera's heart bubbled with conflicting emotions. For one, she had learned to live with loss and grief. Utterly heartbroken for the people she had lost, and left behind. Like Jenna, her best friend. On the other hand, she had a burst of gratefulness for the way her supernatural existence had turned out. Choosing evil had given Sera the identity she had always wanted. Even more so, needed. Her choice to embrace her inner demon had benefited her beyond measure.

Yet, a discomfort stirred in the depths of her soul, churning deep inside. The pulsating energy she had long ignored wouldn't let her do so now. The essence of who Sera was, the new and unique person she had become, had been pushed down for far too long. It was about to take her over.

Halfway to their parked car, Sera suddenly stopped. A

knot formed in her gut. She bent in half in agony. Damon grabbed ahold of her so she wouldn't fall. Sera moaned in pain. She couldn't speak in any decipherable words.

"You'll get through it," Damon said.

He rubbed her back. People passing by shot them looks of disgust. He sent the firestorm in his eyes back at them, and they high-tailed it away. Groans escaped from somewhere deep inside of Sera. It was as though a hand had reached inside of her, squeezing, twisting and turning until she couldn't hide it any longer. She arched in pain, barely able to get out a breath, let alone speak clearly.

"What the hell's happening to me?" She muttered between gritted teeth.

"It's normal after a transformation," Damon whispered near her ear.

"It's been almost a year. How's this normal?"

Tears welled up in Sera's eyes, both from the physical pain and fury from being caught off guard. She slid to the ground and pushed her back up against the wall of a storefront. With her knees pressed up against her chest, she hoped she could hold her insides in. She feared they were going to come out of her.

"It's the completion of your metamorphosis. It happens after a hybrid transformation. However, it can take a long time. I'm not surprised yours happened in your first year."

She barely heard a word of what he said as she was now rolled up into a ball in agony on the ground.

"Why didn't you tell me this was going to happen?"

"I wasn't sure it would happen at all." Damon reached to help her up. "I never met an Ensoul hybrid before."

"I can do it." Sera pushed off the wall, trying to slide up into a standing position. "You could have at least warned me such a thing was possible. Something..."

She moaned as another pulse of pain rolled through her.

Damon grabbed her hands to pull her up. He tried to place her arms around his neck.

"You won't be able to walk on your own."

"I'm all right. You don't need to carry me."

"I didn't want you worrying about when it would happen and what it would feel like. The anxiety alone would have driven you nuts."

"Hold onto to me." She clutched his arm. *I'm strong. I'll get back to the car on my own two feet.* "Walk beside me, like you always do."

Damon didn't argue with Sera. Instead, he steadied her as she gently put one foot in front of the other. Hunched over, she was still able to walk on her own. When they stopped for a moment, so she could get her bearings, Damon pulled her hair back and twisted it into a flat knot on her neck.

"Anyone who says demons are evil never met you." Sera touched the diamond wings on fire around her neck as a reminder of what they both were now.

Right as they passed the last alleyway before reaching their car, she could breathe a little better. The pain was subsiding, becoming more manageable. An unsettling feeling nudged her. Strong enough to make her halt dead in her tracks. All of Sera's senses went on high alert. She hadn't felt like her old human self in a long time, but this was entirely different. An infinitely sharper version of her, one that belonged only to her, like a second layer of skin.

Without thinking or understanding why, rage replaced her agony. It was a far cry from the anger she experienced while living as a human being. It packed itself tightly into every cell in her body. Sera couldn't resist the urge to attack. She ripped her hand away from Damon. Suddenly, she felt a pull down the dark alley ahead of them. She instinctively had to follow her gut.

As Sera ran, she heard Damon's voice. It was far off in the

distance as her legs moved with a mind of their own. She sprinted down the alley until she reached the place where she was most needed.

Leaning against the building's brick wall was a young man dressed in disheveled in dress and in soul. He flicked the ash from his lit cigarette, then physically tore into a husky at the end of a leash. He burned holes into the dog's skin as the animal whimpered, backing away with each attack. Sera's sudden appearance interrupted him.

"You got a problem, bitch?"

The man pulled his arm back as if to burn her with the cigarette. She smiled as she approached him, responding to his profanity with a calm voice and demeanor.

"I may be a bitch, but you're the one with the problem."

He huffed at her and spit on the ground. "I got no problems."

He stared at her as he kicked the dog hard in the ribs. It shrieked. She didn't give him a chance to blink. As fast as lightening, she tore the leash out of his hand and secured it around her wrist. His expression showed his confusion as to how Sera had relieved him of the leash so quickly.

"Lady, what do you think you're doing?"

"I think I'm doing what your dog here would do if she had thumbs."

"Huh?"

Sera got close enough to smell the stench of his unbathed body. She gently wrapped her fingers around his pockmarked throat and squeezed.

"Get off of me! Do you know who my father is?"

The wicked tone of Sera's laugh shocked her. "Your father? No, I can't say I know who your father is. But my father, well, some people call him Hell on earth. Others call him the leader of all demons."

She blinked her eyes with intention to change them from

their usual teal hue to a demon's opalescent color. It was one of the tricks she had learned to do as soon as she transformed into an Ensoul.

"Oh, shit. You're a demon." The former bully turned into a jellyfish beneath her tight grip. "Let me go! Help! Someone help..."

Sera squeezed harder until he could no longer speak. "There's never going to be any help for you. I'm sorry to say it, I am. In fact, there's no help for you on earth, or wherever it is you're going now."

"Don't do this. Please—"

He couldn't finish his sentence because Sera had cut off his airway when she lifted him up off the ground. He was taller than her, so it made no sense how she was able to pull off such an act, but she did. She held him far up into the air until he began to choke from the sheer force of her hand.

"Like I said before, you're the one with the problem."

Sera turned her hand in a sideways motion with unfathomable force. In an instant, she had snapped his neck. Sera opened her hand and let the man's dead body crash onto the unforgiving concrete. She stomped hard on his ribs.

"That's for hurting the dog, asshole."

With a terrified husky in tow, Sera headed steadfastly toward Damon. He waited patiently for her on the main drag of Red Reef. When Sera reached him, she turned back to witness the aftermath of what she had done. No guilt followed her. No sadness filled her chest. In truth, she felt better than she had felt in all of her years, living and otherwise.

"Meet our new friend."

"What's her name?"

In a knee-jerk reaction, she responded.

"Hope."

WHEN THEY GOT HOME, THEY GAVE HOPE A BATH TO clean her wounds that would never heal. Burn scars covered her fragile body in a sadistic tattoo mosaic. No matter, she was beautiful to Sera with irises as light as a demon's eyes. Hope was exactly what she needed. Sera might have saved her, but Hope had saved Sera right back.

Lying in their king size bed, the husky wiggled her way in between them. Only for the first night, they had said.

Sera's mind wandered as she stroked Hope's back in a caressing manner.

I'm a killer. Pure evil. She smiled.

"What's going on in that dark mind of yours?"

Sera grinned. "Tonight was perfect."

Damon laughed. "Wow."

"Wow, what?"

"I never expected to hear those words, especially not after what happened."

"What? You didn't think I could handle this supernatural life, did you?"

Damon turned to her, in all seriousness. His words drifted deep beyond her, landing inside of her soul.

"I knew you would be more than all of us together. I had no doubt you would surpass every stereotype, transcend every obstacle in your way. I've always believed in you. Don't ever doubt my confidence in you. Not even for one second."

Sera pulled his words straight into her heart and held them there, tightly.

"Then, what's so shocking?"

He raised his eyebrows and paused a beat before answering. "I never imagined you would get to a place where you finally believed in yourself."

He held her face with both hands and kissed her hard.

Sera was caught off guard but fell into his embrace with ease. She never wanted to let him go. Their life, in that precise moment, was exactly as it should. It was everything she ever wanted, and all she ever imagined; sheer perfection.

Damon pulled away from her. "I'm happy for you, my love. I'm so incredibly happy for the both of us." He looked at Hope, squeezed between them. "All of us."

The three of them fell back on the bed, entangled in a comfortable embrace. Sera prayed it would never end. Fantasies didn't last forever. Sooner or later, reality would catch up to them. Still, she was grateful. It was good enough for her.

Sera closed her eyes as she drifted off to sleep.

I was born to live in darkness. I've got a lot of work to do.

CHAPTER 9

Damon caressed Sera's lower back as he walked with her down the long corridor to Lorenzo's office. Sera fondled the diamond wings on fire pendant swinging from her neck.

"Do you think she's okay at home all alone?" She asked

After last night, Damon was certain Sera would have been in a better place, especially when it came to a dog.

"Hope has a better life than most people."

"Did you put the music on?"

Sera acted as though he had let the dog roam the streets while they were both at work. Damon halted mid-step and turned to regard her.

"The classical station is on like you suggested. Now, would you please relax?"

Sera bit her lip. "I heard it calms them."

"Well, then you did the right thing. Hope will be okay, I promise."

He had never seen her like this before. Damon held her gaze until her expression showed her agreement. Sera took a deep breath and stood a little taller. Damon gave her a gentle kiss on the head.

"That's my girl. Stay focused. Don't let him see you like this."

"You're right. Hope is fine."

"She's better than fine. She's yours."

Damon escorted her into Lorenzo's office. He was sifting through a few papers on his desk.

"Right on time, as always. Have a seat, my dear. We'll get started in a few moments."

Damon walked Sera over to her chair. He whispered in her ear, "You can do this."

Lorenzo chimed in. "Of course she can. She's my daughter."

Damon smiled a goodbye to Sera and turned to leave. As he exited, Lorenzo called to him, never lifting his gaze from the computer screen.

"I'm expecting those quarterly reports today. It would be best if you closed your current position on a high note before taking on all the difficulties of what lies ahead."

Damon hadn't written a word of his reports. He had no idea how Lorenzo had known. He had never needed to remind Damon before. Why now?

"You'll have them by day's end."

He closed the suite door behind him, sending a silent wish for Lorenzo to take it easy on Sera today.

Once at his desk, Damon got right into his work. Lorenzo didn't ask for typical company quarterly reports. Damon's assignment consisted of compiling up to date investigative notes on each of the senior managers working for Enzo and Dell, and a few other key personnel. As a result, he spent most of his workdays in the office behind a desk tracking the executive team's online activity. After hours, he followed Lorenzo's elite department home where he reviewed surveillance footage. Each vice president was personally audited around the clock with only a select few, Sera included, aware of it.

While Damon's marketing title was Vice President of Internal Audit, he had no financial or accounting knowledge in his background. Nor did his job consist of any tasks a hired auditor would perform.

Damon's experience came solely from doing criminal investigations when he worked as a detective. It was no secret Lorenzo's company was largely a cover-up for demon affairs, but he still had to ensure the business itself was a legitimate operation. His company was expected to fit in with the rest of society so he could conduct his dealings without unnecessary interruption.

In truth, Enzo and Dell was a high-powered law firm filled with crooked attorneys, human and demon, who manipulated the legal system. They had offices all over the world, but the home base was located in Red Reef, New Jersey. The Jersey Shore was also where the most powerful demons resided and dubbed demon headquarters.

It made sense for the principal players to be headquartered in the Red Reef office, including Lorenzo's vice presidents and those with access to the most confidential and restricted data. A local director ran each of the regional offices, domiciled in major cities around the world. Lorenzo wasn't as concerned with their loyalty because he held each office head accountable for the behavior and performance of their staff, in and out of the office. If an employee slipped up, the regional director always took the blame. The structure kept his leaders honest, who in turn ensured their people stayed on track.

Despite few issues over the years with employees who couldn't be trusted and were subsequently *terminated to Lorenzo's mortal standards*, operations ran fairly smoothly. His business model was simple, with some exceptions...demon leaders always held higher-ranking positions than their human counterparts. The organizational structure wasn't only how he ran his business, but how he planned to rule the world one day. And soon.

Damon logged into his private server where the confidential information was downloaded from all over the world. He let it do its magic. When it was done importing the new data, he opened the master file. He renamed it for the third quarter of the year. After clicking on a few options, he immediately began making edits to update the file. The only people missing from the list of employees were Damon, Sera, and Lorenzo himself.

When Damon completed his initial work, he clicked to run the investigative program. It was an in-house build designed to identify any red flags in the region offices. A red flag would prompt a second look and a possible call to the area director. Depending on the complexity of the issue, an investigation would be done to determine which employee was at fault and to understand the gravity of the damage done. If it was a personal slip up causing the flag, Damon always found a way to make the infraction work related. Without fail, the issues came back to job performance, and the employee was subsequently reprimanded, up to including termination of his or her life. Also, the director paid gravely when they didn't hold up their end of the bargain. Lorenzo didn't tolerate mistakes in any of his dealings with either humans or demons. He couldn't afford to give second chances.

A few minutes later the file stopped running. A few red flags appeared on the screen. Damon opened up each of the identified records, digging deeper to find out the issues. One was flagged because the Miami receptionist also had a part-time job as a stripper. He cleared the flag. Lorenzo had no issues with strippers unless they were involved with drug dealers. Drug dealers were known to be predominately anti-demon or demon hunters themselves. Damon would have had no choice but to address the issue with extreme action. One thing Lorenzo was passionate about was demon rights. He also had zero tolerance for anyone who didn't respect and honor his supernatural race. Drug dealers weren't the only humans notorious for anti-demon behavior. Anyone who did time in prison was also a concern. Having no social network when they were released, ex-cons were quick to pledge their hate for demon kind. They quickly gained consensus amongst their peers, which helped them tremendously in other areas of their lives. The problem Lorenzo identified with the prisoners and ex-cons was they never realized the real demons were the faces staring back at them in their own mirrors.

After triaging all of the regional flags, Damon was confidently able to report he found no issues of significance. He gave all of Lorenzo's offices a seal of approval for the third-quarter.

Next on Damon's list was analyzing the headquarters' files. In addition to compiling the in-house records, he also had to sift through hours of video before he could provide his final report. It was the part of his job that took the most time and discretion.

During the tedious task of analyzing the videos, Damon spotted Owen Smith. The onsite techie guru was precisely the staff member Damon needed. He called Owen into his office, gesturing for him to approach the desk.

"How was Florida?"

Owen pushed his glasses on the bridge of his nose up. He shrugged his *pencil-pushing* shoulders. "Grandma's out of the hospital and back at home. I'm going to use my vacation time to visit her for the holidays."

Even though Owen was human, Lorenzo had given Owen

a role with more access to secured information than any other human being in his organization. It boggled Damon's mind how Owen had taken his highly administrative function as seriously as if Enzo & Dell were his own company. To Damon's benefit, however, Owen was always eager to lend a helping hand. He never realized he wasn't helping Lorenzo. Damon was aware once push came to shove, he and Sera would need Owen on their side.

"Great news." Damon pretended to click a few things on his computer screen before asking for help. "Hey, I need a favor."

"At your service."

Owen curtsied in an awkward manner. Damon tried not to laugh at Owen's overly theatrical movement.

"I need you to restore my access to the shared executive drive. I can't open it from my laptop for some odd reason. It must be a network issue."

Damon shook his head and feigned searching his computer for the drive that no longer existed. The shared executive drive consisted of files only accessible by the company's demon leadership, Owen and Lorenzo. Unbeknownst to Owen, Damon had figured out how to use the drive to gain access to Lorenzo's files. Damon normally had access to a regular shared executive drive. But when Owen performed the second layer download to refresh Damon's laptop, access to Lorenzo's files would appear. To Damon's benefit, they remained there for a few days. Owen likely had no idea, since he never took action to secure the temporary link.

"A simple refresh should work." Owen smiled broadly showing his crooked yellow teeth.

"Excellent. I have reports due to Lorenzo today, so I need it to be expedited."

Owen nodded briskly. "Sure thing, I thoroughly understand. Don't worry, Mr. Serpe. Your full access will be restored in under an hour."

Owen gave Damon a goofy salute and shuffled away. Damon shook his head again. He didn't understand how one human being could be the epitome of a geeky stereotype down to the nasal inflection in his voice.

Damon decided to take a look at Owen's video file out of sheer curiosity for the life of a certified nerd. Damon hadn't ever had a problem fitting in. His good looks coupled with a calm and serene demeanor made it even easier. He was like a chameleon. He found people like Owen a rare specimen in a world where humans spent most of their time getting others to like them. Damon had no intention of finding anything damaging, but he could use some entertainment at the moment, especially with all of the seriousness facing him in coming days. He also didn't want to run the risk of watching the clock all day worrying about Sera's training.

Damon pulled up the file labeled *Smith, Owen* and pressed play. Popcorn may not have been needed for any of the employee images, but Owen's record was as benign as they came. Every single day he had the same exact routine. At six o'clock in the morning, Owen left for work. At six o'clock in the evening, Owen arrived home from work. The guy never left the house but to go to Enzo and Dell. It made no sense.

Damon shut his file down and opened the confidential file of the person he was most interested in spying on.

CHAPTER 10

Sera challenged the ruler of all demons with her gaze. Confidence was all she had to offer, knowing he was about to test her to the edge of sanity. Lorenzo presented with a business-as-usual demeanor, her offensive tactic not deterring him.

"Good morning, my dear. Are you ready for our session today?"

His salt and pepper hair temporarily distracted her. Was it dyed, or would she, too, age in her supernatural state? It wasn't supposed to happen, but then again, nothing was as it was meant to be thus far. She had so many questions about being an Ensoul but her supernatural origin was not what training day was about.

Sera twirled her hair around her finger. Her nerves had overtaken her confidence. She folded her hands in her lap nonchalantly.

"Let's get started." She leaned forward in her chair.

As if on command, the double doors to Lorenzo's office abruptly opened. Gina Iona walked into the room carrying a tray of beverages. As Lorenzo's Executive Assistant, she handled everything from calendaring his appointments to picking up his dry cleaning. It was perfectly reasonable for Sera to see Gina carting around drinks like a cocktail waitress. Her long red hair was secured in a tight bun on the crown of her head. Her petite figure had the appearance of being a few more inches tall. Her slim black and white fitted mini-dress along with her patent leather heels made her resemble a server from a posh bar and or restaurant.

In fact, she was serving alcohol. Alcohol being offered at an eight o'clock morning meeting confused Sera. Perhaps it was part of her training, or to calm her nerves. It made more sense to her than social consumption of booze at such an hour. After Gina placed a goblet in front of Sera and a small glass in front of Lorenzo, she promptly left the room.

"No offense. I like my wine, but I can't handle it this early in the morning."

"Under normal circumstances, I would agree with you. But this is no ordinary situation." Lorenzo held up a vial of clear liquid up and regarded it. "This here is a stellar breakfast supplement suited for world leaders."

He poured half of it into his drink and swirled it, to blend. He stretched his arm out to pass the remainder of the vial to Sera. She waved her hand at him.

"I'll pass for now. Maybe later, after I've had my lunch."

"Nonsense. It's perfectly safe, at any time of day. In fact, you've had it before."

Lorenzo reached for her glass and tipped the vial into her drink. Sera pulled her glass toward her. She pushed away from the table, readying herself to stand.

"I'm sorry. I thought you insinuated that you previously drugged me?"

"Drugged is such a harsh term."

Lorenzo made a tsk-tsk sound and went back to admiring the vial. He smiled in apparent wonder at magnificence Sera could not see. It looked like clear liquid and nothing more to Sera. Still, she didn't want it in her drink. She didn't wish to drink anything at all.

"So you admit it?"

"It significantly helped your progression along. No need to thank me. It was my pleasure."

Sera's mouth dangled open like a participle with nothing to support it. "I have no intention of thanking you...ever."

"You can't say it with confidence, my dear. There are things you don't understand yet. And, I assure you, you will be grateful for all I've done, even if not today."

"Grateful? You put me under the influence of who knows what, causing my insides to turn themselves inside out and, not to mention, my snap judgment murder."

Sera clamped her jaw shut, as to not allow any more words to fly out. She pulled her crossed arms closer to her chest, holding onto her rage before it took on a life of its own. If there was ever a moment in time to hear an explanation for something, it was at that precise moment. But, Sera wasn't about acquiescing, at least not with a smile.

"I also healed you. You're choosing to forget that part."

Sera recalled how she had felt in the hospital after those demon hunters had attacked her. The clear liquid called Blaze had done more than heal her. It had made her stronger than she had ever been. She had no intention of admitting this to Lorenzo, at least not yet. First, she needed to understand what plans he had in store for her. More importantly, how his super-secret liquid played into it all.

Sera relaxed and slid her chair back under the table. "Alright, then. Go ahead. Tell me all about it. What's in the vial?"

She had been curious. Now was as good of a time as any

for her to find out what had made her into a *super demon*. Lorenzo didn't answer her at first. He acknowledged her willingness and interest with a brief grin. He, again, began examining the remaining liquid he held.

"I named it Blaze, but I discovered tetrodotoxin's effects a few years ago when I traveled to Haiti. Yohan requested a trip home as his bonus, and so I thought, *what the hell*, and joined him. I've always loved to travel around our great planet. There's beauty and mystery in so many things, especially when it comes to the supernatural. Humans are so wrapped up in themselves to notice and appreciate what they can't understand." Lorenzo shook his head. "Nevertheless, while Yohan was busy visiting his family, I took it upon myself to sign up for an exotic fishing excursion with a handful of locals. There, I began to learn the intricacies of the ancient Haitian voodoo culture. Their obsession with death wildly intrigued me."

"How so?"

"The Haitian culture is much more evolved than you might think. Haitians have a thorough understanding of the line between life and death. Dare I say, they have a grasp of the ways of the supernatural? You can't help but respect them for it, particularly where we stand in this world. Notably, they use the natural environment around them to cross over to the other side, and to come back."

Sera shivered. "This texa...where does it come from?"

"The puffer fish excretes the poison known as TTX."

"Bizarre."

"It is hard to believe." Lorenzo laughed. "Haitians are smart, don't ever underestimate any one of them. They used the poison regularly in an ancient ritual. In the correct dosage, TTX temporarily transforms human beings into living zombies. They are as close to death as they will ever be, barely a pulse. Yet for all intents and purposes, they are still alive."

"Sounds like it could kill a human."

"The right dosage of anything could take a human's life. Too much water in too short of an amount of time would do the trick."

Had the liquid been given to her in a pill form when she took her own life? She supposed anything was possible.

"Even with a completed death, crossing over to the after-life isn't ever their goal. They have bigger plans. They want to perfect the art of suspending life in an altered state for a period of time. Of course, there's much more to it all. But when I learned this, the wheels in my head turned. You see, what started out as a vacation, quickly transformed into a research trip. Many excursions and experiments later, I became convinced TTX would change the world for us."

"Such a powerful statement."

"For a potent drug like Blaze, it is accurate. It's a synthetic version of TTX, more powerful and less expensive to produce than the real poison. It works better, too. As you know already, it makes demons stronger than we've ever been before. Even more so for you and I, as Ensouls. I haven't determined its full power yet. When I found out how those dreadful human demon hunters attacked you, I gave a vial of Blaze to Dr. Winston at *Demon General*. I explained how it worked and how its existence wasn't to be shared with anyone unnecessarily. He takes his position seriously and understands the consequences of betraying me, so I wasn't concerned. Winston assured me he would administer the drug to you himself to prevent it from getting into anyone else's hands. And, as I anticipated, it healed you. Thanks to all that is evil in this world."

Sera allowed his revelations to simmer for a moment. She tried to understand what he was attempting to accomplish and how it all fit together. When she put the pieces in order, she was sick.

"Your intervention at the hospital wasn't the only time you ensured I ingested this Blaze, was it?"

Lorenzo shrugged as if it was nothing. "I had no doubt it would heal you, but I had to see what else it would do. I hoped you would have the same reaction I anticipated on the second round. To be sure, I had to see it with my own eyes."

"You've been experimenting on me all week long?"

"Now, now, Sera. Calm down. It's all for the benefit of demon kind. No harm was done to you. In fact, you've progressed into your supernatural state nicely. As a result, we're ahead of our timeline. You are finally ready for the next level."

"Next level? You drugged me for your purposes. Without my permission. I can't express to you enough how much I do not appreciate being treated like a lab rat."

She stood to leave. She had had enough of Lorenzo's devious manipulation. Lorenzo waved her to sit.

"Sera, please. I'm not here to hurt you. You should know that by now. I have big plans for you. For us. It's why you're here with me today."

"Then be straight with me. I need to be able to trust you. I can't go around worrying about you drugging me whenever you feel like it. If you want me to stay, to be on board with all you have in store, you need to tell me the truth."

"Fair enough." Lorenzo motioned again for her sit.

She obliged, reluctantly. "Tell me about the other night."

"When I dropped Blaze into your champagne, I wasn't doing it to harm you in any way. For one, it was diluted. For two, I was aware how it would make you feel superior, which is they way you should always feel. It was time for you to truly become who you were always meant to be. And, I was betting on Blaze to accelerate your progress. Suffice it to say, it did that and soon after digestion. I was very pleased."

Sera clenched her hands into fists. His audacity was more than she could handle, but she had to march on. She pushed her hands onto her lap as to not do anything she would soon regret.

"You saw me?"

"I couldn't have been prouder."

Lorenzo glowed with satisfaction. Nausea settled in her gut, along with the reality of the life she had chosen for herself. A supernatural psychopath was not only her boss. He was her father.

"Your proudest moment was watching me snap a man's neck, killing a human being because I could not control my fury, nor my hunger for murder?"

"Indeed it was."

Sera was disgusted, but not surprised. She should have known better. No amount of artificial kindness or figures in her bank account from Lorenzo would change the evil incarnate inside of him. She had no choice but to set her personal feelings aside if she was going to survive successfully as an Ensoul. Her focus needed to shift. Sera had serious work to do. Time was running out.

"Let's get back to why I'm here."

Like an actor playing a role, Lorenzo put on his business face, the one with no expression. "Make no mistake about it. You and I, and all of our demon cohorts are preparing for an all-out war between the supernatural race and the human race. It is us against them, Sera. The old adage has never changed."

"You know their concrete plans?" She pushed him up against a wall, and she knew it. Lorenzo wouldn't attack her directly, nor would he tell her the whole truth. She needed to get as much out of him as she could.

"We are the ones with the concrete plans. I know it's not what you wanted to hear, but it's the truth. We must be prepared. If we are not one step ahead of them in our strategic objectives, then it will be too late. Before we know it, we will have fallen prey to the human race once again. And precisely when we turn our backs, right when we lie safely in our beds at night, they will hunt us down and take away our lives as if we were fleas on a stray cat. I, for one, am not going to become another nameless victim. And, I won't allow you to become one either."

He navigated the conversation like a champion chess player. Sera needed to make her next move.

"If you're being honest with me, then what can I do to help? "

Lorenzo's face brightened. She had done her job.

"That, my dear, is better served shown versus told."

He placed the vial on the table between them. While she may not have had a choice of being a part of him, Sera could decide to never to be anything like him. If superhuman strength were what he offered, she would take it. It was exactly what she needed to defeat him.

Sera grabbed the vial. An expression of pleasant surprise marked his face. She paused over her glass, teasing it. A brazen confidence bloomed exponentially inside of her. It bordered on excitement for what was to come. She had taken a leap of faith when she underwent the life-altering metamorphosis a year ago, dying as a human being to be reborn as an Ensoul.

What are a few drops of liquid going to do to me?

She tilted her head, smiling at the man who had birthed conflict in her heart. It was time to take him on.

"Any last words of advice?"

Lorenzo took a moment to examine her before he responded. "Embrace the real you."

The low tone of his voice unnerved her, as if he knew better. Sera wouldn't let him manipulate her. She had to remain in control. Sera dumped the remainder of the vial into her wine and raised it high above her, in a grandiose toast.

"Here's to me." She swallowed the contents of the glass in a single gulp.

CHAPTER 11

Damon's door flung open. Xander Klein sauntered into the office looking like he didn't have a care in the world. Because he never did.

"Yo, Day. Wanna grab some beers after work? Maybe some apps, too?"

Xander was an oversized goon, in Damon's opinion, who was more suited to become a linebacker on a professional football team than to run an operations department. However, his brawn often came in handy and would even more so as a soon to be demon leader in the future *New World Regime*.

Damon pressed stop on the file. He switched to a blank word processing document to be safe. He had to remember to close his door when he worked on Lorenzo's coveted quarterly reports.

"Not tonight. I promised Sera a date night with wine, dinner...the works."

Damon had no formal plans with Sera, but he also had no intention of getting beers, appetizers, or anything else with Xander. Sharing the details of the night, even though they were lies, was Damon's way of telling Xander there was no chance in hell he could make it. He had a way of manipulating people into saying yes when they really meant to say no. The man didn't give up when he wanted something.

Xander's eyes lit up, even though he had missed Damon's message entirely. "Great. I'll tell Hay we have double date. Let me know where and when."

Sera never wanted to double date with Xander and Hayden. His knack for pushing his own agenda, and shortening everyone's name into one syllable, made Damon want to punch him in the face. He often questioned how many brain cells Xander had bouncing around in his gigantic head.

"Sorry. Like I thought I said, we'll have to pass. Maybe another time."

Damon wanted it to be no other time, but it wasn't possible given their shared leadership roles under Lorenzo. Xander stood there for a moment processing Damon's words.

"Sure thing, bro." Xander shrugged and left, his oversized body thumping down the hallway.

Damon quickly shut the door to his office. He needed to get back to working on the files without meaningless interruption, or he would never have his reports done in time. Back in the saddle, he hit the play button and let the entertainment begin.

If any video was worth watching, it was Xander's file. He always had a party of some kind, inviting people over like it was his full-time job. The man never stopped socializing. Sera and Damon were repeatedly invited over to his house. Unless it was a required work event, they always declined. They never wanted to get too close to people given the complications of being in the unpredictable Lorenzo's constant line of sight. Avoiding video evidence of their actions was top on Sera and Damon's list of priorities. They needed autonomy and privacy more than anything in a world where everyone was a pawn in Lorenzo's chess tournament.

Damon leaned back in his reclining leather chair. He lifted his feet up onto the desk, stretching out to watch the rest of the video. He laughed to himself, thinking how it was entertaining.

Xander's house was a revolving door of visitors. His girlfriend Hayden came in and out on a regular basis, which was to be expected. There were a few guys Damon didn't know who frequented his home, but they looked like thugs to Damon exactly like Xander did. Also, another couple of coworkers, the last people Damon would have guessed enjoyed spending time with the jock. They popped in and out over the weekend nights.

To each his or her own.

Finally, Damon saw something concerning. He hit the pause button.

A truck with no lights pulled up a few doors down from Xander's house. It parked on the opposite side of the street. The act itself wasn't completely out of the ordinary until he saw a small, dark figure dressed all in black sprinting toward Xander's front door. A lock of long red hair stuck out from underneath the baseball cap as if it were put on in a rush and not tucked in entirely.

A woman in disguise. She was jittery, rebalancing her weight from foot to foot in her stance, as if dancing. Repeatedly she looked around with jerked head movements. She was obviously looking to see if anyone had spotted her.

Damon zoomed in on the figure and paused. The military style fatigues. Tall boots. Oversized gear. It was the story he didn't want to hear.

Xander had lost his half-baked mind.

Damon made a note of the timestamp on the video. Almost midnight on a workweek. He hit the play button again and paid close attention. The second the door opened, Xander threw himself into in a sensual embrace with the woman, practically dragging her into his house.

Damon didn't watch the inside video on the same day. There was no need. It was clear what was going on. Instead, he fast-forwarded through the remaining days in the quarter on Xander's tape. Every few days going forward, the same girl in black showed up, and the similar scenes played out in front of the video. Xander was cheating on Hayden.

Even worse, the mistress was a demon hunter.

Damon shut off the video and sat upright in his chair. Head down, he ran his fingers through his hair. He had no idea what to do with the information he had learned about one of Lorenzo's most trusted leaders. What was Xander thinking? He wasn't. And it would cost him everything.

Damon wasn't sure if he should confront Xander directly to get the facts, or if it was better to reveal what was on the tape to Lorenzo without confirming the truth with Xander first. Damon wasn't even certain if he should tell Sera what was going on. He didn't want to keep anything from her any longer. There had been enough lies between them in the past. However, he also didn't know what kind of risk he would be putting her life in if he shared Xander's betrayal with Sera.

It didn't matter that Xander was cheating on Hayden. Most assumed he was doing it on a regular basis anyway. What mattered was that he was having an affair with a demon hunter. He wasn't only betraying Hayden, he was betraying all demons. Worst of all, he was double-crossing Lorenzo. An act their ruler wasn't going to take lightly.

Lorenzo treated all demons working under him, except for Sera and Damon, equally. However, in this situation, Xander had a leg up, literally, over the rest of them with insight and exposure to the other side...their mortal enemy, the ones who would rather torture demons than come to an agreement on how to live together.

Hunters were the reason the war was coming.

A part of Damon felt sorry for Hayden for a second. Then he didn't. She was as stupid as Xander. It surprised him she could keep a smile on her face as long as she had with Xander at her side. She was beautiful, popular, and successful. He was a complete dope in every definition of the word.

Of course, he had no way to know Damon would see his demon hunter affair play out on a video. Xander never considered proof of his betrayal might be broadcast for all to see. If he had, he never would have done such a thing. At least he might have tried a little harder to cover it up. Regardless, it had taken place, and Damon was aware. Lorenzo would be expecting a report today. He knew Xander's house had been under surveillance and if it came out that Damon didn't reveal what was so obvious to anyone watching the video, Lorenzo would question Damon's loyalty. It wasn't an option.

The problem was if Xander was in a relationship with another woman, even if she wasn't a demon hunter, the mystery woman still might know more than any other human about everything, including Lorenzo's plans. This, however, was more than dangerous. It was downright demon suicide.

Maybe it was only sex. Damon decided he would have to tell Sera what happened later in the evening. If it were exactly as he suspected, he would need her in on everything so they could work together. On the flip side, it could also be Lorenzo's way of testing Damon's loyalty. In such a case, he would need to keep it from Sera and tell Lorenzo right away.

An alert on Damon's laptop kicked him out of his wavering with how to proceed. An email from Owen popped up on his screen advising him the files he previously requested were ready to be downloaded.

After all that had happened, it wouldn't be safe for

Damon to view these particular files while in the office. He pulled the small flash drive out of the interior pocket of his blazer and plugged it into the side of his laptop. He clicked quickly through the file folders until he got to the tenth level down. The files he wanted were hidden within a folder marked as temporary. He copied the entire contents onto his flash drive. The download took a few minutes since there were almost three gigabytes of data in the folder. After it fully transferred, Damon correctly ejected the flash drive and stuck it back into his blazer pocket, out of site. He closed out of all of his files, shut down the auditing program and opened up the Internet for good measure. He would take a look at the details later after he got home and was safe on his personal computer.

Damon decided he would say nothing about Xander in his quarterly report for Lorenzo. If he questioned Damon, he would admit what he saw but state it was information he didn't want to document via email. He would tell Lorenzo he preferred to discuss the sensitive topic with him privately when they were alone. Once Lorenzo found out what Xander did, it would be disastrous for all of them. By dating the demon hunter, Xander had jeopardized any secrets he had. This would put all demons at risk if they were shared with anyone. There wasn't a good outcome for Xander, or any demon if details about their plans leaked out into the general public. Damon had to come up with a strategy, and fast before the entire situation got out of control.

He spent the next few hours finishing his formal report until it was ready to be delivered to Lorenzo.

A pang of worry about Sera in her training hit Damon, but there was nothing he could do about it. Sera had to go through the motions and handle whatever Lorenzo threw at her. She didn't have much choice. Time was running out. She needed to be fully trained and ready to go for when the *New*

World Regime was thrust into place against humankind's will. Even more so, now that she was Lorenzo's second in command.

No matter what the outcome, they would fight back for certain.

CHAPTER 12

A warm breath gently tickled Sera's cheek. She rubbed her eyes until they opened. The owner of the blurry face peering at her was barely recognizable. After blinking a few times, Lorenzo's assistant's fire engine red hair came into full view.

"She's awake," Gina said.

Lorenzo's voice seemed miles away when he was only across the room. "Get her settled first. Then we'll begin."

"Supernaturals pass out a lot, huh? No one warned me about this when I was human." Sera sighed.

Gina giggled. "Fainting has nothing to do with being supernatural. That's all you."

"Awesome." Sera shifted her body so she could sit up straight.

"Here, let me help."

Gina slipped her bony arms under Sera's torso and lifted her into a seated position. The assistant was surprisingly strong for her slight size, which made sense because she was a demon. Those violet contacts and proper demeanor always threw Sera off. Gina looked and acted so perfectly. It was as if she was almost human.

"I'm good," Sera said.

She hoped it was true. Although, she felt like she imagined someone who had snorted cocaine might feel. Her thoughts and emotions flew around the speedway in her brain on endless loops. No finish line in sight. The energy and flood of desires bounced around inside of her like fireflies in a jar. Trapped with no way to escape. The insanity multiplying in her brain should have made it impossible for her to focus. Sera's mind was as sharp as a guillotine. She was ready to lop off the head of any villain in her path.

Lorenzo approached Sera slowly. "Welcome back to us, my dear."

Sera rubbed her eyes. She searched for a clock somewhere in the room, but didn't find one. She didn't own a watch. The only jewelry she ever wore was the wings on fire necklace.

"How long was I out?"

"Not very long at all. I'd say it was about fifteen minutes. Right, Gina?"

"Barely." Gina shrugged.

"It's impressive given the amount of pure Blaze you ingested. I'd planned on giving you a droplet, not the entire vial. I wasn't certain of your reaction since it's generally taken in a diluted form. I thought we might have to ride this one out and wait for another session later on when the dosage could be controlled. You seem to be in perfect shape."

Sera beamed with pride. She had surprised herself. "I'm as perfect as I'll ever be."

"Superb. Then, I suppose we're all ready to get started. Gina, take over. You will lead the exercises from this point forward as we discussed."

"As you wish."

Gina handed Sera a tablet and stylus. She had no reason

to dispute Lorenzo's method, but she was curious. She had an inkling it wasn't going to be as simple as her answering a few questions and going on her way. Nothing up until that point had been simple in her life, whether human or Ensoul.

"What can I expect from these exercises?"

"With most of the drills, we'll know immediately if you pass or fail," Gina said.

"Pass or fail? I thought this was a training session. Not a test."

Sera was confused. She hadn't anticipated her ability to fail. What would failure possibly mean for her supernatural future? Knowing Lorenzo, succeeding was the only option.

The pressure was on.

Gina wore a cunning smile. Her eyes darkened. "Both. With the other tests, we'll be using a unique and innovative electronic device to capture your data so we can analyze it further later."

"My data?" Sera had no clue what she had gotten herself into. She had nothing to say about a technology she didn't understand.

"Let's get started."

Gina pointed what looked like a remote control toward a far wall in the room and pressed a button. As the sheetrock opened up, it gave way to a large concrete room. It was one Sera hadn't seen before. The area looked more suited for bulk storage versus a hidden office space. In the center of the otherwise empty room, two men sat comfortably in high back armchairs. They wore similar attire...denim jeans, simple crew-neck shirts, and sneakers. They looked like they were having a casual conversation.

Except their ankles were chained to the floor.

Holding people against their will wasn't part of the Sera's plan. Outrage surged her. A pitcher of water flew off of the conference table and smashed into the wall clear across the room, shattering all over the carpet. Sera jerked back.

"What's going on?"

Gina's eyes grew wide. "Well, well, well. It looks like you've already passed the first test. Congratulations!"

Lorenzo raised his eyebrows. "Notable and impressive. I'm not surprised."

"Recording the details now, Sir."

Gina typed on her tablet. Sera's gaze darted between them, searching for a sensible answer.

"What test? We didn't even start yet."

Sera had no idea what they were talking about. It wasn't as though she told them about her anger. Instead, it swarmed her, without a conscious thought in her mind. Gina promptly educated her, as a teacher would with a student.

"It's self-explanatory. You manipulated a physical object with your mind. It's the first test on my agenda to administer today. Yet, I didn't have to do a thing."

Gina smiled at Sera as if she had done her a favor. Sera was happy she had made Gina's day easier, but what she had said was completely incorrect.

"No, I did not."

Sera was adamant. She would have known if she had done something so deliberate and dramatic. Sera wasn't the type of person to knowingly make a statement with her behavior, let alone do it without knowing.

Lorenzo stepped closer to Sera. "Your emotions and thoughts are much like mine. They have a physical power. They're alive. You haven't mastered them yet, but you will in time."

Sera contemplated what Lorenzo said about her propensity for power. It reminded her of the other night when her emotions had driven her to save Hope, and to commit murder.

Sera pointed to the glass-strewn floor. "I did that?'

Gina nodded as she click-clacked away, never looking up. "Lorenzo's right. We need to work on your focus and your intent. But for now, we can cross telekinesis off the list."

Sera sat with the word telekinesis. Never in her wildest dreams did she imagine moving objects with her thoughts and emotions. Sera tilted her head in the direction of the chained men for another explanation. If she was to pass any more tests, she needed to understand the game and the players.

"What are they doing here?"

Gina smiled knowingly. "They're part of your exam."

"Chained against their will?"

"Chained, yes. But not against their will. They've given their full consent to this experiment. They'll be paid handsomely in return for their services."

"If you say so," Sera said.

Gina turned toward the men. "Tell her, boys."

The men shouted in agreement with the services for payoff exchange. The ankle chains still bothered Sera, but she had no say in her training or testing program. She supposed there was a multitude of situations where she would have to turn a blind eye if she wanted to survive in her supernatural world. Like the restrained men, Sera had made a decision that brought her to this exact place in her life. In doing so, she'd inadvertently agreed to whatever was to come her way in exchange for the life she wanted.

"What's next?" Sera asked.

"We'll test your mind to mind abilities for both species. Human and demon."

Gina lifted her hands in the air at the men. It must have been a signal letting them know it was okay to get off the floor and take their seats. The training, the test, whatever they wanted to call it moved too fast. Sera hadn't been given an opportunity to gain control. She had flown through the training by the seat of her pants. Exactly the way Lorenzo wanted. The challenges seemed to be administered in order of complexity and importance. If Sera showed them nothing more regarding her ability, one of the two things could happen: Lorenzo would think she was useless and since he was powerful enough, he would have no need for her any longer. Or, he would know she lied, essentially betraying him. Then she would be in real danger.

Both options sucked.

"Since all demons can read human minds when they concentrate, tell me what the human person in the room is thinking. Lorenzo and I will be able to confirm instantly."

Sera heard his thoughts immediately. The human's identity was no longer a secret. It was a tidbit she would use in future exercises.

"Gina has an incredible ass."

Gina blushed. She approached Sera with an odd device resembling a headband with a tiny wireless box attached.

"For the rest of the exercises, you'll be wearing this data collecting headband."

Not knowing what data they would be stealing from her brain niggled at her. She was about to be exposed. Her most intimate thoughts would be on display.

"What data does this headband collect?"

"Your brain waves. Along with any other means of communication you're sending out. Even ones you don't even realize exist. All the information will be directed to a program designed to translate these complex signals into actual words to be analyzed."

"Huh?"

"In other words, this device will download your thoughts."

Sera's worst fears had come to life. They would be downloading data directly from her brain, revealing her innermost thoughts. She wasn't fantasizing the worst—the worst was happening. Technology had advanced to the point of downloading one's thoughts? Amazing. And terrifying. She didn't think such a technique was possible. Yet she had no doubt if it were, Lorenzo would be the first in line to utilize it. A reality that was disturbing in and of itself.

"So what you're telling me is...you're going to read my mind?"

Sera would never be able to make her brain waves lie. Yet how could she refuse the headband? The shtick was over. She would have to accept defeat. No one was strong enough to overcome both drugs and a supercomputer at the same time. Not even a demon...Ensoul...whatever the heck she was.

"And you'll read mine."

Sera slipped the device onto her head, adjusting it until it was comfortable. Of course, it was a perfect fit.

"I didn't know such a thing was possible."

"That's what we're here to confirm."

Gina closed her eyes and relaxed her shoulders. In a brief millisecond of clarity, Sera knew exactly how she would play their game. Her next move was a dangerous but essential survival tactic. She went for a gold medal.

"Let's see. At first, you thought what a ridiculous exercise this was and how no supernatural being could read another supernatural being's mind. But if you wanted to keep your job, you would have to go along with Lorenzo's unreasonable requests. Another thought squeezed its way into your mind— that you were happy someone finally noticed your great ass because you've been working out for years and no one has ever said anything about it to you. Next was the thought you wanted me to hear, which was how you do not like green eggs and ham from that ridiculous children's book. Finally, you were glad you weren't ever going to have any children. You can barely afford to take care of yourself on your hellacious salary, and with all of the horrendous things Lorenzo makes you do, surely he could give you a raise—"

Gina interrupted Sera. "Well done. Telepathy of a human. Passed. Telepathy of a demon. Passed. As you know, these powers are unique to Ensouls. Therefore, you share these abilities with Lorenzo. And Lorenzo only."

Lorenzo gleamed at Gina's words, gloating over his superior offspring who was created in his likeness. He looked like a deity towering over his God-fearing people. From there on out whatever Sera accomplished was all gravy to him. She had passed his all-encompassing test.

He needed her.

"Next, you must manipulate the physical body with your mind. I'll give you a command via our shared program. You'll mentally project it toward these handsome men so they can complete the task as you have suggested it to them. Take your time. Most importantly, remember to concentrate."

Sera's heart pounded out of her chest. It was one thing to pass a test she didn't know she was being given. But to be presented with a specific goal she had to achieve? Impossible. She passed once by reading a demon's mind, but the expectations would continue. How would she continue to do exactly what was asked of her with no time to prepare?

The notification popped up on her tablet. Sera read it. Before she had a chance to direct her attention to the men, let alone look their way, they shot across either side of the room, their chains ripped away. Sera's gaze bolted from the tablet and volleyed between the men and Gina. All three were agape in awe. Even Sera was impressed with the scope of her powers.

Lorenzo got up from his seat at the far end of the conference table slowly. He made his way to Sera's side of the room until he was within feet of her.

Gina cleared her throat. "Physical manipulation of the

human body. Passed." She paused for a beat. "Physical manip-ulation of a demon body. Passed. As you should already know," Gina continued matter-of-factly, "demons do not have the ability to control one another."

"I do." Not surprising. Sera's powers as an Ensoul were beyond those of demons.

Gina swallowed hard. "However, as you may not know, Lorenzo has related that Ensouls also do not have this ability."

Sera had demonstrated an Ensoul power she did *not* share with Lorenzo. Her stomach gurgled in nervous confusion. It had been confirmed. She was more powerful than Lorenzo. Sera glanced at Lorenzo to gauge his reaction. She expected denial but got something else entirely from the ruler.

"Brilliant." Lorenzo clapped loudly. "Bravo. Bra-vo!"

Surprised at his reaction, Sera smiled in return. She hoped her display of overachievement would be enough to prove she was worthy of Lorenzo's genes. Especially since it was all of the abilities she intended to show them, if she had her way, except for her willpower.

For the next few hours, Gina put Sera through a series of tests examining if she could probe deep inside of the demon's mind. Gina wanted Sera to delve into the hired demon's memories and attempt to see into his future. She ventured a guess she could do all of those things since it took every ounce of her focus to stay on point and blank out her mind, which seemed to be working on overdrive.

For the human portions of the test, Sera used all of her energy, even though it wasn't necessary. She drained it for a second, which was enough to still her mind for the demon portions. In the end, it took all she had inside of her to deceive the headband of horror. But she did it. And prayed no one was the wiser.

After Sera had failed a few consecutive exams, Gina and

Lorenzo lost interest. They had their data. They thought they knew what Sera was capable of as an Ensoul. Lorenzo had what he needed to forge ahead with his master plans.

For Sera, it was a turning point. The naïve human girl turned clueless supernatural being now had enough knowledge and power to save the world.

It was exactly what she intended to do.

As soon as Lorenzo released her, Sera went home and hit the bathroom to freshen up. She looked horrendous. A mirror wasn't needed to prove it, but she peeked into one anyway.

Her hair, formerly coiffed in loose waves, fell in strings around her face from the sweat caused by stress. The makeup she had taken so much time to perfect was smeared as if she had been standing out in the rain, face to the sky. Her clothes were wrinkled and she was battered from head to toe, much like her spirit.

She patted her face with a wet towel, then flattened her hair, pushing it behind her ears. A few spritzes of perfume, some compact powder, and lip gloss cleaned up her broken look.

Moments later, Sera flung Damon's office door open. When he caught sight of her, he shot up from his seat and ran to her side.

"What did he do to you?" His voice was as low as it had ever been.

Sera put her hand up to collect herself. Tears fell. No words escaped her. Damon grabbed her close to him. He held her tight. His chest heaved rapidly next to hers. Sera thought he might fall into tears, something he had never done.

"It was me. I did this." Sera's voice was barely audible. She could hardly get the words out. All of her energy and emotions had drained out of her completely.

Damon pulled away to take her in. His eyes scanned her face. "He did something to you. I know he did. What was it?"

"Lorenzo didn't do anything to me. My abilities did. They're so much more, so much stronger than I ever imagined."

"Of course they are," Damon said.

"You don't understand. I'm more powerful than our ruler." The words sat with Sera. She embraced them like an old friend.

He spoke in a reassuring tone. "Don't worry about what he has seen. I'll take care of it. Everything will be all right."

An unanticipated rush of joy overcame Sera. A tear fell down her cheek, but it wasn't from pain, sorrow or defeat. Her tear was born of victory. She smiled, gazing into those protective eyes, and told Damon the truth deep within her heart.

"He saw exactly what I wanted him to see."

CHAPTER 13

Lorenzo reveled in his daughter's powers. He knew from the moment Sera was born she would be in his likeness. It was precisely why he had to have her in his regime.

"I'm surprised she's still standing." Gina shook her head in amazement.

"I had no doubt."

"She's remarkable," Gina said.

"Mental strength of any kind is not to be underestimated, especially from an Ensoul. More so from *my* Ensoul."

He had always been the only Ensoul. Now he spoke confidently about Ensouls as a species since there were two of them.

"An Ensoul such as Sera."

"Even Sera is not exempt from the challenges she will face in coming days. Bring me up to speed. What are we dealing with here?"

Gina opened her tablet. She swiped through the test results on the screen.

"If you would have said she could physically manipulate a

demon yesterday, I would have thought you were delusional. I knew we were testing her for outrageous abilities, which I assumed would be at your highest level. However, I never expected her to surpass your abilities as an Ensoul."

Lorenzo straightened. "One. She passed one test above my Ensoul level."

Gina rolled her eyes at Lorenzo. "You would have to be blind if you think that's all she's passed."

Lorenzo glared at his insignificant assistant. Disrespect was not rewarded. Especially not from his most loyal followers.

"I hope you take your elite position at Enzo and Dell seriously. You know as well as I do there are hordes of demons who would give up all of eternity to be seated at my right hand."

Gina collected herself, evidently realizing her misstep. She replaced her smirk with a plastic grin.

"Of course I am. I'm beyond grateful for the opportunities you've given me."

"Alright, enough with the brown-nosing. I must admit, she was extraordinary."

His face grew warm as he thought of Sera. He had only a small hand in what made her a physical being, but he had no problem taking credit for all of it.

"She was a diamond in the rough today."

Gina's expression reflected a loving glance as if she were in awe of his offspring. Lorenzo snapped himself out of his gloating demeanor.

"Enough with the compliments. Tell me your expert evaluation of the session."

Sorority girl turned statistician, Gina flipped through a few screens on her tablet until she reached the complex chart Lorenzo wanted to analyze. She spun it around to present a quasi-formal account of Sera's data. Gina used her stylus as a pointer.

"As you can see here, Sera passed fifty percent of the tests, ten percent of which were not expected since no other being on earth has been known to possess those abilities." Gina refrained from theatrics this time, using a reserved tone.

Lorenzo massaged his jaw. "Understood. What else?"

"Of the fifty percent of the tests she failed, the results were...inconclusive."

He cocked his head. "You must be mistaken. How could the test results be inconclusive if you're also telling me she failed them? Do you not understand how to read the data?" He stared her down, demanding an answer.

"I can explain." Gina's face twitched as if she were holding back a sneer. She swiped the stylus until the chart turned into a grid with pinpoint-sized dots.

"What are you waiting for?" Lorenzo was as impatient as he was rude when things didn't go his way.

"You can see precisely where she has passed. The left side of the grid indicates a supernatural being and the right side indicates a human being." Gina locked the view and turned the screen sideways. "As you can see here, the top of the grid is indicative of supernatural abilities, while the bottom is reserved for human abilities." She looked up at him for acknowledgment.

"Don't patronize me. Just go on."

"What I'm showing you is an example of one of her tests. Keep in mind this grid is designed to depict true results, whether we can understand them or not. Take a look over here." Gina put her stylus on the screen where she wanted Lorenzo to focus.

"What am I looking at?"

"See the many tiny pinpoints spread out on the left-hand side of the screen? They're also above the baseline."

Lorenzo squinted in concentration. He was a strategist who simply never had to pay much attention to numbers, as someone else always analyzed critical metrics for him.

Gina seemed to sense his unease with the details. "To be perfectly clear, the baseline would be where we would expect a regular demon's score to fall. As an Ensoul, we would expect her to fall farther left than a normal demon and higher above the baseline as well. A human, for instance, would fall into the far right bottom of the grid. Whereas a regular demon might fall somewhere in the middle of it all, underneath the baseline. It's not a straightforward mathematical formula, but it does tell a story."

Lorenzo huffed, frustrated with the nitty gritty. "Tell the story faster. I'm losing concentration with your dots and grids and jibber jabber."

"I'm getting there. Stay with me."

Lorenzo tapped his fingers on the desk. "I'm going to smash the tablet through the window if you don't hurry up."

"For each independent test, Sera's results were much like this and exactly what we would expect. She had more points on the supernatural and ability side than a typical demon, which is how you fair. However, when we combine them together..."

"And...this means what?" Lorenzo asked in an annoyed tone.

Gina paused to show a final screen of all results in one place. "We see how on the whole, Sera is completely off the charts, in the literal and figurative sense."

Lorenzo stared at the diagram. The puzzle pieces were finally clicking into place, connecting to the big picture. He leaned in and pulled the tablet from Gina's hands, demoting her from teacher to student. He needed to get a closer look.

Gina was exactly right. Sera's pinpoint dots clustered together in the far top left portion of the grid. Some of the dots went clear off the page.

"Son of a devil. How can this be?" He shook his head.

Gina adjusted her glasses. "In my estimation, either her abilities are still hidden from her..."

"Or she is powerful enough to hide them from us both."

Lorenzo let his conclusion settle on his lips. He licked them to taste the implication of his words and denied them in his next breath. A flamethrower ignited in his mind, and he jerked upright.

"I doubt that," Gina said.

"We need to retest Sera."

Gina's gaze darted around, obviously uncomfortable with his request. "I'm not sure if..."

Lorenzo put his hand up, cutting her off. He leaned into her, his tone hard. "I'm not asking you what you are sure of, Gina. I'm telling you we need to retest her, and soon. However, this time she must be caught off guard entirely."

"Sir, we have never done anything like that before. I'm not sure how..."

Lorenzo's forceful glance shut her up. "There's a first time for everything. Send the reports to me when you get back to your desk. You're dismissed."

Gina scrambled to gather her things. Halfway to the door, she turned around as if to ask a question.

Lorenzo had responded before Gina had the chance to speak. "I'm working on her final exam. You'll get an email about it shortly. I'll expect you to take notes."

Gina stuttered. "But...I don't know what we'll be doing."

"Or alternately, I could post your position as a new opening. I've received many resumes this month. Some looked impressive."

Gina straightened. "I'll be there with sequins on."

ॐ

AFTER GINA LEFT, LORENZO SUMMONED OWEN SMITH TO his office.

"I've been waiting for you." Owen had several notebooks in tow as he sat opposite Lorenzo.

"Perfect. Tell me what you've found." Lorenzo tapped around on his computer, half paying attention to his nerdy human employee.

"You're not going to like it." Owen wiped the sweat from his brow.

Lorenzo stopped typing mid-sentence and turned to hear Owen more fully. "I'm not? Now you have me intrigued. What is it that I'm not going to like?"

"It's Damon." Owen dropped his head in shame at his delivered news.

Lorenzo hit the desk with his fist to grab Owen's attention. "What about him?"

"He's not to be trusted." Owen's voice trembled.

Lorenzo's voice came out like the deep roar of a lion. "What you're suggesting isn't acceptable. I'll need proof of your accusations."

"He saved the temporary video files onto his personal flash drive. The spyware program download is in your inbox." Owen stuttered the betrayal, then let out a deep breath.

Lorenzo's tongue rolled over his teeth in contemplation. He turned on his computer. Owen, a human with no defenses, knew better than to assume anything when it came to Lorenzo. He had made sure of it when he hired Owen as the company's mole.

"If you're wrong and I take action...I don't have to tell you what that means for your position or your life."

Owen pulled his inhaler out of his pocket and took a breath. "I wish I was wrong, sir."

Lorenzo clicked on his email link. He immediately spotted the note sent from Owen. There was a file attached, the one Owen had promised exposed Damon's betrayal.

"I'll take a look on my own. You should stay on top of your assignment and keep me informed if any more information comes your way. Understood?"

"Yes, sir. I understand entirely. I'll make sure you have whatever you need."

Lorenzo made his way next to Owen. "You're dismissed. I'll see you out."

Owen waddled to the door, dropping his head in shame. Lorenzo locked the double doors behind his techie spy. Privacy was crucial. He couldn't afford to be interrupted. Once seated comfortably in his oversized recliner, Lorenzo double-clicked on the email from Owen. It was blank. All he had sent was the file. *Smart boy*. Lorenzo double-clicked on the file. It opened up. His screen filled with data, much of which was useless to him. He scrolled meticulously through Damon's computer activity.

Lorenzo was pleased to learn Damon had seen the video with Xander. It was meant to give Damon something to chew on. It could possibly even put a wedge between him and Sera. If Damon didn't tell Sera, she could always read his mind once she got control over her powers. The truth always came out. Lorenzo hoped Sera would keep the tidbit about mind reading to herself, but it was highly unlikely. Even so, it would cause them great turmoil to consider how to handle Xander's affair with a demon hunter. Pressure on a relationship during a fragile time in their lives could push them right over the edge. He could dispose of Damon with no hard feelings. Sera would have nowhere to turn except to her dear old dad.

Lorenzo laughed at his simple brilliance.

He clicked on a few other files until he landed upon the

one he needed. Exactly as Owen said, Damon had downloaded the entire file onto a flash drive.

The real file sat on Lorenzo's personal netbook, never accessing a network with the potential to be breached. He popped open his mini laptop and reviewed his master plan. While he didn't need it in writing, he loved seeing his words come to life on the page. His plans were more than he had ever dreamed they would be. Chills ran through him at the future exposed on the screen before him. He knew nothing could stop him from achieving his goals. Had he been equipped with emotions to evoke tears, he would have cried endlessly in joy. This mission and vision had made him more powerful than ever. If that was even possible.

With Sera by his side—and he was still confident she would be—the world and everyone in it would be his puppets.

Lorenzo sent an email to his Red Reef office. It would determine if his dreams with Sera would come to pass. He announced an unassuming last minute outing. An afternoon off of work to reward his staff who worked diligently to make him the success he had become. The perfect cover for an emergency meeting and a pre-test for his daughter, who had done a superior job in the face of adversity.

Whether she intended to please him or to deceive him, they would soon find out.

CHAPTER 14

DECEMBER 25, 1993

The happiest and most frightening day of Rafaela's young life had nothing to do with the holiday.

She slipped into the bathroom unnoticed as Lorenzo watched the annual Christmas Day football game. It was only the two of them. She wasn't feeling well, and Lorenzo never had a problem staying home. For a few minutes, all she could do was lean against the sink and tremble. She was terrified beyond comprehension at what was to come next.

Lorenzo and Rafaela had never been careful. In fact, they had been notably laid back in their relationship for two reasons: one, no communicable diseases had ever been transferred, sexual or otherwise, between humans and demons; and two, it was impossible for a demon to impregnate a human. To them, it was a win-win situation.

In turn, their relationship bred passion and excitement. Rafaela and Lorenzo were free, nothing held them back.

Still, Rafaela had always felt their freedom was limited for reasons she couldn't put her finger on. It gnawed at her gut. She tried to push it out of her mind, but it often crept in without warning when they were intimate. Without any proof, Rafaela couldn't help but feel they were wrong about what was possible and impossible.

The day before, Rafaela had purchased a pregnancy test at the grocery store. She was three weeks late, and while it could have easily been attributed to stress, since it wasn't exactly easy to date a supernatural being, Rafaela was convinced otherwise.

Over the past week, the first thing Rafaela did every morning was vomit. It was something to take notice of, even if it didn't make sense to her. Since it couldn't be pregnancy, surely she was dying of some terminal disease, like cancer or the plague. Either way, something wasn't right with her.

Rafaela needed an answer once and for all.

She took a second deep breath, knowing whatever the outcome might be, the array of emotions would be nothing less than life changing for both of them. Whatever the test results brought, be it happiness, relief, sadness or regret, there was no way for her to win; pregnant equaled freak, and not pregnant equaled childless woman, which most still considered a freak.

It was sheer torture for Rafaela to wait for those damn lines to appear. Or not appear. She felt like she had held her breath underwater for too long and might drown at any second. Rising to the surface of reality couldn't come soon enough. The impossible outcome had nothing to do with interspecies reproduction. Rafaela's gut feelings made no scientific or logical sense but all the sense in the world to her.

She rubbed her belly waiting to confirm what she believed in the depths of her soul to be true.

Rafaela strode quietly out of the bathroom. She barely uttered a sound when she sat next to Lorenzo.

After a few seconds, he glanced her way. She began to rub her midsection in a circular motion.

His face twisted in confusion. "What's wrong?"

"Nothing." She smiled.

He shrugged and turned back to the game.

Rafaela cradled her stomach in the best way she could, given it was still flat as a board. She leaned in to her love. He peered down at her, his arm around her, when she saw his eyes finally land on her hands below.

Again, he was utterly perplexed and nearly brushed it off. Until he didn't anymore, and that's when he pulled away.

His eyes told her everything. He knew.

"Impossible."

"Not impossible."

After staring at her for a few moments, he rose abruptly, almost dropping her to the couch, and began pacing. His questions flew around the house in a tornado, not directed at either of them, but swirling into the universe.

"How is this possible?" He scratched his head. "What does it mean?"

Rafaela held her breath. Would his reaction be a normal one like happiness or anticipation? It was neither. He approached her announcement like an astrophysicist might approach a new theory on time travel. Joy combined with confusion were the mixture of emotions Rafaela couldn't reconcile.

After Lorenzo's attempt to reconcile the strange news, he and Rafaela went about their usual evening routine, attempting to avoid the subject at all costs. They both knew the questions weighing on the other's mind. They were having a baby, but what would it be? Human, demon or something entirely different?

Lorenzo looked as if he had aged ten years in the last few hours. It seemed as though wrinkles had grown around his eyes and brow, deepening by the moment. While demons didn't age, as far as Rafaela knew, she was certain his face hung a little heavier. The reality drifted between them like an offensive odor. People would soon find out a demon had impregnated a human.

If reproduction between two species was possible, wasn't anything?

When the word got out, life would never be the same for either of them. When the silence sat too heavily in the room, Lorenzo left.

Thirty minutes later, Vera came over in response to Rafaela's frantic call. She filled her best friend in on the pregnancy. Vera's reaction was not one of happiness but one of worry.

"Oh dear."

"Okay, that wasn't the reaction I expected. So, what is it you aren't telling me?"

When Vera didn't look Rafaela in the eyes, she knew her best friend had held back crucial information about the pregnancy.

"You don't want to know. But you need to know."

What Vera revealed next sent Rafaela's mind spinning until the entire world as she knew it fell completely apart.

Nothing would ever be the same again.

CHAPTER 15

PRESENT DAY

Sera was ready for the fight of her life, yet also surprisingly relaxed. The luxury bus Lorenzo had chartered for all of his supernatural employees at Enzo and Dell was super comfy. Even though they were only driving five miles from their Red Reef office to the beach. An afternoon at her favorite place and away from the one that challenged her the most? Perfection. Exactly what she needed.

Damon squeezed her leg. "Hey there. Don't get too comfortable. We're technically working."

"Why not? I haven't had a good sleep in a couple of nights. Oh, and not to mention a pack of demon hunters attacked me. Of course, don't forget I was also tested for all umpteen levels of my supernatural brain capacity. That kind of stress can leave a girl a little tired. Some shut eye won't hurt anyone, will it?" Sera closed her eyes again.

"Like I said, this isn't a day off."

Sera opened one eyelid and peered at her man. "Don't underestimate me...or forget how my naivety died with the rest of my first name."

"Touché. Sweet dreams, my love."

❦

WHEN THE BUS PULLED UP TO THEIR DESTINATION, SERA felt like her eyes had only been shut for a few seconds. She wasn't far off. The bus ride had only been fifteen minutes.

"Rise and shine, beautiful." Damon nudged her.

Sera yawned and stretched her arms, releasing the tightness in her biceps.

"You're a first-rate comedian."

"Someone needs to keep our spirits up."

"Speak for yourself. My spirit is perfect."

Sera pushed the button on her seat. It flew upright. She wiped the already trying day from her eyes and gathered her energy. The bus halted to a full stop about a half a mile from where beachgoers played. When its door creaked open, Lorenzo walked to the front by the driver and turned around, taking command. He clapped and whistled loudly to get everyone's attention.

"We're here, people. Let's make our way onto the sand. Instructions will follow, as usual."

A collective sigh fell among the staffers, now realizing they were attending a work-related event when they mistakenly assumed they had been given an actual day off from work. A stream of random demon thoughts bounced around the bus as well as in Sera's mind. Feelings of strong discontent with the current situation surfaced loud and clear in her brain.

Lorenzo stepped off of the bus first, clearly ignoring the visual disappointment on his employees' faces.

"Here we go," Sera said.

She stood with the rest of the crew, following their fearless demon leader out of the bus and onto the beach. Lorenzo led the reluctant group over the dunes. Once they assembled, Lorenzo grabbed Sera's hand. He pulled her front and center next to him until they were both facing the others. Sera absolutely hated being the main object of attention. Unfortunately, it was the norm in her new world. She would have to get used to it. And fast. Another necessary evil if she wanted to be best suited for her elite Special Demon Forces leadership role in the future New World Regime.

Damon waved to her in a breezy way. She wanted to flip him the bird but smiled broadly instead.

"Contrary to what all of you may think, this is not a team-building excursion. After my first and only demonstration, you will, indeed, have the entire rest of the day off."

A wave of cheers came over the crowd. They quickly turned their attention to Sera, Lorenzo's demonstration.

Sera was curious and a little nervous. Given their intense session, the word *demonstration* had new meaning. It meant pure torture.

"As you know, our supernatural lives are in grave danger as of late. We are all well aware demon hunters have existed as long as we have, and they have never stopped wanting to destroy us. This fact—well, it's not a brand new concept by any stretch of the imagination. However, today's statistics regarding the increased demon hunter population are, quite frankly, striking." Lorenzo paused for effect. "The Jersey Shore Association for Spiritual Science published a recent article stating that the percentage of humans who have a friend or family member who is a demon hunter has risen from eight percent last year to nearly fifty-four percent this year."

Collective gasps tore through the crowd of demons. The statistics even amazed Sera.

"Shocking, I know. And those numbers are only representative of the Jersey Shore area. The statistics don't even begin to touch upon the rest of the state, the country, or even the world."

There was a quiet hush. One of the girls from accounting yelled out, "We're screwed."

Lorenzo laughed. "To say the least. But you don't need a math degree to understand these are uncertain times for our kind. And as I mentioned recently, we have no choice but to take severe and stringent action."

More shouts of support rang out. Sera was embarrassed at how everyone fell so quickly in agreement with Lorenzo no matter what he spewed out. No facts were checked. They blindly believed him.

"Now for the reason we're here as opposed to a bar, which is my favorite place. Sera, my dear, sweet and beautiful daughter."

Hoots and hollers rang out, but Lorenzo's attention focused on Sera. Everyone else's attention focused on her, too. As Lorenzo's smile beamed at her, so did the darkness behind his gaze. Sera feigned embarrassment for the attention, shoving the distrust settling in her gut far below the surface. Lorenzo paused a moment to admire his daughter, and then quickly turned back to his crowd of minions.

"With the ways of the world being so cruel recently, our friends are turning into our enemies right in front of our faces. As such, it's crucial we're all publicly adamant about where our loyalties lie. We must prove vehemently beyond a centimeter of doubt whose side it is that we're on."

Murmurs during Lorenzo's speech turned into silence on the heels of his words. While the vast majority of his followers were loyal to the death, many of them drifted out on their own when they weren't in his presence. They had their questionable moments of forced independence. Lorenzo had turned a blind eye to their actions because they were his leaders. And, truth be told, none of them had outwardly aligned themselves with humans in any way. Their individual betrayals had been a deadly secret reserved strictly for the hearts and minds of Sera and Damon, a fact of which Lorenzo could not possibly be aware. Still, fear and unease were evident in all of their expressions. They didn't want to be questioned regarding their loyalty, knowing death was the only resolution to such a problem in their leader's eyes.

Beads of sweat trickled down Sera's back. The sun was no match for the rampant anxiety building within her. She tugged at the side of the black trousers hugging her hips, attempting to mask her distress in a benign casual act. Her demeanor had to be strong, confident, and up for whatever challenge came her way. Sera took a deep breath and smiled wide.

"For this reason, it's only fair that my own child is held to the same standards as I've held all of you to in my regime thus far. Recently, I announced Sera as your new leader in our Special Demon Forces as well as my second in command in the New World Regime. She, too, shall be forced to prove her loyalty, not only to me but also to all of you."

Lorenzo didn't mention her abilities or her sweeping test results. Clearly Sera wasn't the only one keeping secrets. She sighed in relief. Lorenzo held her hand as he spoke aloud to her, facing the crowd.

"Are you up for the challenge?" he asked.

This time, Sera took control. She raised their hands in the air in unison, a former gesture he had forced when she was promoted in front of the same crowd. It was a visual representation of how she was now united with the team. She spoke the words she had to force herself to believe she meant.

"Let's do this."

The crowd roared and clapped, obviously relieved for her to be the demon put on display. Sera's eyes drifted between the shoulders and heads bobbing until she was able to catch Damon's gaze. While he was smiling from ear to ear, the sentiment never reached his eyes. The only emotion she saw on her lover's face was utter despair. Either he knew what was to come for her, or he had feared the worst imaginable alongside her.

Lorenzo beamed. He seemed pleased with her new attitude.

"Let's give my daughter a hand."

The demons cheered and clapped. Sera beamed right back at them because it was expected.

"I appreciate your support."

As she held the diamond wings on fire in her grasp, she heard her mother's words once again. *Beware of the truth.* A moment later, Lorenzo took off, leading his people in a march down the Silver Lake shoreline. Sera followed a step behind Gina, who was always at Lorenzo's side.

Sera drew in a deep, sea-salted breath, contemplating the place she loved more than anything. The beach was her tainted lover, and she, its mistress. A bittersweet love affair she couldn't escape, painful and therapeutic all at once. Her one saving grace in times of trouble, the shore was where she had gone to process her father's death. It was also the place where she had learned her family friend, Vera Olivio, who had revealed Lorenzo to be her biological father, had been killed. Now it would hold the memory of where her loyalty would be tested, something she had struggled with since she metamorphosed into a supernatural being almost one year ago.

Sera pressed on, keeping pace a few feet behind Lorenzo.

"You were amazing up there." Hayden Rosen, who was not only Xander's girlfriend but also Sera's quasi-friend, fell into step next to her, getting in on the action. Hayden was the most popular employee at Enzo and Dell. It was no surprise why. She was stunning, bright, a go-getter, and a wonderful person to everyone she encountered. Most importantly, she was loyal. Loyalty, while rewarded when it came to Lorenzo, was hard to find in the demon community otherwise. Demons were liars who loved to break all the rules.

Sera hadn't let anyone get too close to her, even though Hayden was someone she liked in her supernatural life. Most others she merely tolerated.

"It was easy. I had a cheering squad," Sera said matter-of-factly.

"You made it that way. You've never shoved your elite status in anyone's face. The daughter of our ruler is a position that was bestowed on you. It's your birthright. You could have used it to your advantage, and no one would have held it against you. Any girl would give up all eternity to be in your position. Yet you act like it's no big deal. It's as if Lorenzo forces you to admit you're something great over and over again. But if he didn't, you would be happy with people thinking you cleaned the bathrooms around the office."

"Maybe not the bathrooms. The mailroom is more my speed. I do have a thing for organizing."

Sharing an ordinary moment with a friend when everything else in her life was as abnormal as it came was so refreshing.

"You could show Xander a thing or two. He doesn't know his left from his right. I swear, when he stays over, it's like a pack of wolves broke in looking for food. The place is a nightmare. My cleaning lady comes every Monday because I couldn't function if I had to live with him."

"When that day comes, I'm happy to help."

"No time soon," Hayden said stiffly.

"Besides his desire to live in a horse barn versus your beachfront townhouse, I thought you guys were close."

"We are." Hayden paused.

"But?" Sera asked.

Hayden looked toward the ocean. "I thought we were... until recently, that is. He hasn't been around much lately. He cancels our plans. A lot. I can't reach him when I really need him. He says he's on assignment with Lorenzo, but I think something else is going on."

Everyone but Hayden knew that Xander was a womanizer. Sera refused to get involved in someone else's relationship. She preferred to focus on a truth that was positive.

"You're everything any man would ever want. No woman is better than you for him."

"There's always someone better. It's how relationships work. We're only around as long as they're still interested."

Sera considered Hayden's harsh words. It was a terrible way to look at love. Perfection wasn't possible. Yet Hayden implied the moment you weren't everything your loved one wanted you to be, it was only a matter of time until they found someone else.

"I disagree. Love is love. If he loves you, it means for both the good and the bad times. Not only when everything falls neatly into place. That's not possible. Real life is messy."

"What you're defining is marriage. This is dating, a phenomenon much more complicated. Besides, who's to say Xander even loves me?"

Sera slowed to a stop. She waited for Hayden to figure out she wasn't walking beside her any longer and turn around. Sera tried to avoid judging, but she wanted to understand.

"After two years, Xander hasn't told you he loves you yet?"

Hayden squared her shoulders in a defensive stance. "I haven't said it to him either."

"You love him, though. Don't you?"

Hayden picked up her pace. "Where do you think we're headed?"

Sera dropped the subject altogether. There was no point

in trying any longer when it was evident Hayden didn't want to talk about it.

"From the looks of it, not far."

Sera pointed up ahead on the beach to where she spotted another crowd forming. They were positioned around a faint outline of a demon's worst nightmare. Hayden's face contorted when she took notice of the scene.

"What do you think he's going to make you do?"

Sera watched as shades of orange, red, and yellow danced in a staccato ensemble, sliding from left to right with the light breeze. The colors of her hell dipped low at times, and at others they were flying high, glints soaring tall into the sky above. They mesmerized her when they should have caused terror. People dressed in black were gathered all around the dance number. Some of them were huddled in what looked like a conversation, while others were engrossed in the lyrical display as if in a trance. Whatever the answer, Sera wouldn't have a choice in the matter. She would have to do whatever Lorenzo wanted and hope for the best.

"I have no idea. But we're going to find out in about fifty feet."

Gina fell back from Lorenzo and into line with Sera and Hayden. "You should be up here with us." Gina's tone was condescending.

"Go. It's your show now," Hayden said.

Sera placed a hand on her friend's shoulder. "We'll talk later."

"Let's go." Gina gave Sera a dirty look as if she'd had enough before heading to her leader.

"On my way." Sera set off at a jog to take back her throne next to Lorenzo.

"There's my woman of the hour." Lorenzo's tone was annoyed.

Sera was out of breath, and out of shape as it turned out.

She needed to justify her actions. The last thing she wanted was to enrage him before he made her prove her loyalty.

"I was chatting with the team."

"Your team can talk to you some other time. Today is about you."

Lorenzo nodded in the direction of the humans all dressed in black. They were engaged in a ritual, and it was one where demons didn't belong and never would.

Before long, his entire regime had closed in on the demon hunters. The soaring flames begged to torch them all to ash.

CHAPTER 16

The demon hunter leader ran across the sand high-fiving each of her team members. They cheered CJ on in response. She was a rock star at the top of the charts. She wanted to ride the high forever.

CJ had called her hunter meeting only last night. Despite the daylight, the bonfire on the beach was wild and brilliant, drawing attention from onlookers on the boardwalk. A weekday gathering wasn't typical, but her orders had been given. She had no choice but to oblige.

Or she would face the wrath of evil.

CJ didn't mind. The negative drama was a welcome place for her dark energy to thrive. She was on a mission to guarantee her team was prepped and ready to kill. Demon hunters were targets now more than ever. They needed to be primed for war. She motioned for her people to gather around the fire.

"Let's get our meeting started. Assigning tasks is first on the agenda. We have no time to waste."

CJ barked at them like a schoolteacher instead of the

head of the powerful militia that she was. Learning how to lead as a trailblazer for a cause extremely close to her heart was a serious matter. She wished she had the guts to use fear to rule her people. She was a softer leader, more of a visionary-type enforcer. Her hatred for demons ran deep, but she never entirely showed that side of herself to her team. For them, she was a confident woman with a plan. The only leader they would ever trust...she made sure of that. Mad theatrics were saved for the privacy of her own home.

Mandy, CJ's second in command, stepped forward pointing down the shoreline. "They're here."

CJ lifted her hand to her eyes. She tried to block out the sun's glare as she looked in the direction Mandy indicated. To her, the group was unmistakable. Not only would she know Lorenzo anywhere, she was also not surprised about his arrival. She had prepared for it. They were coming, of course, but her hunters weren't in on the secret.

CJ swung around to the crowd behind her. She summoned her decision-maker demeanor.

"Listen up. Lorenzo and his team are headed our way."

Not everyone knew Lorenzo personally like CJ. She made sure her team was schooled in the ways of the demon regime and organizational hierarchy. Growls and gasps worked their way around the fire.

"We're not here to fight. At least not today. If we mind our own business we shouldn't have any trouble at all."

The pack of demons headed toward them wasn't a threat. Her job was to play along while reassuring her team of the same. A few of CJ's demon hunters grabbed the wooden sticks they brought as legally approved ammunition. They headed toward the fire to dip them in, creating instant demon-killing weapons.

CJ commanded in a harsh tone. "Stop it. This isn't the

message we want to send. We're in no position to have a battle out here on the beach in the middle of the day. We need to save our energy and our rage for when the actual war begins."

Mumbles of profanity escaped from a few. While other hunters kicked the sand with their heels and stomped around. They wouldn't disrespect her outright, but they weren't pleased with her decision at the moment. Their understanding would come later. They would need to sit this one out.

"Hang tight. I'll handle this." Mandy patted CJ on the back.

"Keep them under control. I have bigger rats to fry." CJ planted her feet firmly in the sand.

"Are you ready for this?" Mandy squinted in CJ's direction.

CJ understood Mandy perfectly. Lorenzo wasn't who CJ feared. She had dealt with him on multiple occasions and had no issue at all. Although a problem with the demon leader was always possible. Demons couldn't be trusted. Especially not their leader. Surprisingly, it wasn't Alex, their Xander, either. Their relationship was forbidden. Lorenzo must have suspected it. He was too smart to be *that* stupid. CJ took their affair for what it truly was...an affair. She wanted more with Alex, but it would never happen. She would not only have to admit that her feelings for demons weren't universal —a fact most hunters would never be able to reconcile—but she would also lose the upper hand in the war.

CJ was selfish, but sacrificing human survival wasn't an option.

What bothered her most, what set the darkest parts of her soul on edge, was another person approaching. The woman she had backstabbed and double-crossed. The girl whose heart would be broken once she knew the truth about CJ. Yet also the same friend who had done all of those terrible things. Now CJ was the one getting revenge. And sweet, long overdue retribution.

The bomb was about to explode in front of them both. No one would survive.

CJ rolled back her shoulders. "Now or never. It had to come out at some point. I might as well face my demons, all of them, right now."

"You're not alone in this. Our support is real. We've got your back," Mandy said.

"Take over for me here. I need to confront my past. In my own way."

Mandy headed back to the unruly crowd behind them. "Settle down. Move back."

Mandy's voice trailed off into the background as she gained control of the hunters, who were on high alert. CJ drew in a deep breath and spun around on her heels. She made sure her feet were planted firmly in the sand and her legs were the pillars of strength she needed. She took a few steps forward and away from her support group, who were gathering around the fire. Her vision wasn't the best, but she could see they were approaching even closer. They stampeded forward with all the rage of a tsunami attacking the shore.

The demons were on a mission. They weren't going after the hunters. They were coming for CJ.

CJ closed her eyes, not only to rest them from the sun, but to summon the strength she needed. She was preparing for what was about to happen. CJ could never be caught off guard when it came to her enemy. The pain and the torture she experienced one year ago came rushing back to her like a tidal wave.

The moment her lids closed and blackness fell upon her.

She let it take her over. Fear and despair followed close behind, swarming around her like a full hive of raging bees. CJ pulled in another deep breath and thought it could very well be her last. She held back her tears of frustration and anger. *Control yourself.* Her hands fisted at her side as she recalled the memories of the unpleasant events in her mind. It played in a constant loop releasing her unbridled rage with a vengeance. The traumas of her past awakened her deepest motivation. She needed them both to survive.

When CJ opened her eyes, she could see each of the demon faces clearly. They were stone cold, heartless bastards contemplating numerous ways to slaughter her. She had been through much worse. They wouldn't intimidate her away from the master plan. Her jaw clenched with determination. She had to stay strong and set a good example.

CJ took off in a fast-paced walk resembling a sprint. She would meet those bastards halfway. With a quick glance back, she pumped her fist in the air. Her team mimicked the gesture. A much-needed surge of confidence rushed her. Lorenzo must have noticed because he put his hands up in the air as well. His group slowed to a stop. The demon leader was going to let her come right to them.

CJ's long red hair back flew back with the wind. Thank goodness she was a far cry from her former self. When she finally reached the group of demons, she abruptly stopped.

"To what do I owe this pleasure?" CJ squarely confronted Lorenzo.

His sly smile gleamed in the sunlight. They shared secrets. But now wasn't the time for acknowledging the betrayal they both owned. Now was the time for action.

"You're a little early with the bonfire. I don't blame you. Today was too beautiful not to bring my fearless leaders to the beach. Apparently, you had the same idea."

"Get to the point, Lorenzo. I know you're not here to mingle with my team. What do you want?"

Her hands flew to her hips. She knew what he wanted. It was all an act.

"A poignant question in such misunderstood times. You really do have the inquisitive mind of a genius. Of course, I want much more than this world could ever provide to me. But for right now, it's a different story entirely. You see, I was explaining to my people how much the world has changed. How demon hunters like you are on a mission of epic proportions. Everyone knows I love a formidable mission and a purpose, even if it's one I don't agree with."

"They sure do," CJ said.

"I do live for my strategic goals. But when those goals involve harming my kind, I don't take them lightly." Lorenzo's expression hardened into a challenge.

CJ spotted Alex standing firmly behind Lorenzo. Her boyfriend stared her down, another act and the response Lorenzo expected. She caught Alex's gaze for a moment and hoped Lorenzo hadn't seen it. He loved having ammunition in his back pocket for when he needed to pull out a trump card. Both of their lives were in danger if the truth came out. She would never admit she loved Alex, but she did have feelings for him. Despite the fact that he was the epitome of what she hated most in the world, she didn't want him harmed in any way.

CJ sneered in Alex's way as a recovery. She let her disgust fall neatly over the entire crowd of demons for good measure. In her visual sweep, she made sure to skip the one person she prepared to confront.

The fire in Lorenzo's eyes was unmistakable. CJ shook slightly with the realization that while it might all be a performance for his sake, she was up against something she had no business trying to fight.

She cleared her throat and stood firmly too. "How can I help you?"

"I'm so delighted you asked! Introduce yourself to my second in command. Although I have a strange feeling you two ladies already know each other."

CHAPTER 17

Sera took a few guarded steps toward the demon hunter and then changed her demeanor. She needed to show her strength, not only for Lorenzo but also for herself.

"Sera, meet CJ, the Maroon County leader of the demon hunters. CJ, meet Sera, my second in command and, proudly, my daughter."

The woman was much more petite than Sera was used to seeing in a demon hunter, much less a hunter leader. The crew behind her appeared to fit their parts perfectly; each one of them was tall with broad shoulders and an athletic build. To be a demon hunter, you needed to have the strength of mind and body. Not to mention, you needed to know how to fight dirty.

CJ was slender yet shapely. Her long, fire-red waves responded to the light breeze off the ocean, enhancing her femininity. Sera thought she looked beautiful at first glance. Her monotone black outfit wasn't a head turner, but it was stylish. Sera's new mortal enemy, CJ, looked like someone who had it all together, and Sera gave credit where credit was due.

CJ rolled her shoulders back. "Sera."

Sera couldn't see her eyes, but it was evident CJ was staring at her from beneath her large black sunglasses. CJ's appearance wouldn't have gone unnoticed if Sera had seen her before, as Lorenzo had insinuated. She hadn't. However, the tinny pitch to CJ's voice was oddly familiar.

"CJ." Saying she was pleased to meet the hunter would have been a lie. Sera may have been a demon now, but she still wasn't comfortable lying.

"Perfectly done. You see, the reason I've brought the two of you together is to make it known where we stand. As I understand, you've been working on that with your team today as well. And frankly, I applaud you for such efforts, CJ."

Lorenzo began clapping. His select group of handpicked elite demons joined in. Sera couldn't make sense of his intentions. If the beach day excursion wasn't a test, what was the point of dragging everyone out here? Everyone on the planet knew demons and demon hunters weren't exactly the best of friends. It seemed useless for him to point it out in such an uncomfortable way, especially when there was no battle ensuing at the moment. There would be a war soon enough, but it wasn't happening right then and there.

"Why, thank you." CJ smirked at Lorenzo.

Something about the way her face changed touched Sera. A subtle sweetness lived behind the cold exterior, one she recognized. It sent a pang straight through her heart.

"As you have a plan, CJ, so do we. I have a strong feeling —call it clairvoyance, if you will—that we'll meet again very, very soon. In fact, I wouldn't be surprised if it were before the weekend was over."

CJ's mouth twitched slightly as if she was holding back her anxiety and fear.

Lorenzo stepped in closer. "Let's not waste any precious time. I think it's best if the truth comes out, don't you?"

Truth? Sera's gaze darted between the two of them. What was Lorenzo up to this time?

Beware of the truth.

Sera couldn't be sure, but she thought she saw CJ's lower jaw quiver.

Lorenzo leaned into CJ. "Shall I do the honors?"

CJ didn't respond at first, staring him down. When Lorenzo began to move toward her face, she backed up a step, throwing her hands up.

"I'll take it from here."

Lorenzo's eyes grew wide. "Impressive. Truly. I never thought you'd find the courage in your heart to come clean once and for all."

Lorenzo's palms faced the sky in an innocent gesture as he fell back away from CJ, slowly and methodically until he was aligned directly next to Sera. She glanced over at him. Arms crossed, his stance shifted to one hip. An undeniably gloating smile was plastered over his face.

Lorenzo nudged Sera. "This is something you don't want to miss."

CJ took a few steps forward and stopped.

"Go ahead. Come closer. If you're going to do this, you might as well go all out, don't you think?" Lorenzo grinned.

CJ paused, then walked straight up to Sera, standing about a foot away from her. Up close, Sera noticed the curve of her face and the delicate look of a child hidden behind the hardened reality of life. Her fair and freckled skin glared in the sunlight, a distinct contrast to the tanned versions of beachgoers meandering about. Sera couldn't help but feel sorry for the woman.

Until CJ slid her sunglasses onto the crown of her head.

Sera drew in a deep breath, stumbling back a step.

Damon, standing behind her, braced her from losing her balance. She would know those gray-blue eyes, the color of her beloved ocean, anywhere. Sera shot spears through Lorenzo with her unblinking gaze.

"You knew about her all along?"

"She wasn't my secret to tell."

Tears welled up in Sera's eyes, a simultaneous natural and unnatural experience. She had no idea demons cried. Then again, she wasn't entirely a demon.

She was an Ensoul.

Sera turned to Damon. He looked as shocked as her.

"I had no idea. I swear to you."

Sera set her focus back on the demon hunter leader. "I don't understand. What are you doing?"

Sera shook her head in utter disbelief. CJ was Jenna. She glanced away for a brief moment, then returned her gaze to meet Sera's eyes.

"I'm not the person you used to know. I'm different now."

Jenna's words didn't match her pained expression. It was obvious her friend was struggling with the rationalization of what she had said moments before.

"Jenna, it's me, Serafi...Sera." Sera reached out to grab her friend's hand, but Jenna snapped it away.

"I'm not Jenna. I'm CJ."

A mask of anger transformed CJ's face. Sera wasn't used to seeing her gentle and loving best friend look so furious. She started to speak but held back her words, unsure of what to say. Apparently, Jenna's traumatic experience over a year ago had changed her in more ways than Sera could have ever imagined. Resentment and fear plastered Jenna's face. It wasn't the time to fix a broken friendship. It was also a test, one she would have to pass if she were to remain in good standing with Lorenzo and the rest of the demons she would lead. Gut-wrenching conflict swirled in her mind and her heart.

"I'm sorry to be the one to reveal this to you, Sera, but there's more to the story. Your little reunion, while sweet, won't pain you so much once you know the truth."

"I thought I already knew the truth."

Sera forced a calm over her mind and emotions. Dead cold settled in and her heart went black.

Beware of the truth.

If learning her best friend was now her mortal enemy wasn't the truth she came to find out, what could it be?

"Unfortunately, that little tidbit of information will need to be revealed at some other time. I plan to take full advantage of this spectacular afternoon." Lorenzo turned around, gesturing for his team to move along. "So, now that you two have begun to get acquainted again, we'll give you the time you need to work on your obvious issues."

Sera was still confused at Lorenzo's timing. "What's this about?"

"Your final exam."

"I didn't do anything."

"Your hesitation was all I needed to know whose side you're on. In the coming days, your loyalty will only grow stronger, being revealed to us all. For now, we must press on. CJ, Sera, enjoy the sun, ladies."

Lorenzo, along with the rest of his regime, strode off. Damon looked back at Sera as he followed close behind their demon leader. Once the demons were gone, Sera regained her composure to deal with the issue at hand.

"Jenna? This is insane. Can we talk?"

"CJ."

"CJ, Jenna, whatever you're calling yourself these days. You're still my best friend. Why didn't I know about this?"

CJ rolled her eyes at Sera. "Why would I tell you anything?"

"Because I saved your life and—"

"You want me to thank you for letting me live after your sick bastard of a demon friend tried to kill me? You should have let me die that day."

"And...because I love you. I've always loved you. You're not only my friend. You're like a sister to me. I don't care if you hate all demons. Hell, I sometimes do. But don't turn your back on me. You know I'm different. This is me talking, Jen. Me. Can't you see through all of this craziness how I'm still the same old Serafina?"

CJ's face contorted until her dainty features grew dark. "You don't know a thing about love. You're a monster."

CJ walked away in the direction of her team. More than anything else in Sera's life that had caused her pain, the word *monster* crushed her. She drew in a deep breath.

"I'm me. The same as I was. Why can't you see that?"

CJ spun around. "Serafina is dead. She died on September 13th of last year. I know this because I grieved for her. I cried, and I cried until there were no tears left. But then I got smart. I decided to do something with my fear, rage and depression. So instead of sitting around like a useless loser, letting demons rule my life, I decided to take action. Against the demon who attacked me, and against whatever you are who killed my best friend. I decided to fight for every girl in the world who had no one left they could trust. You didn't save me, Sera. Serafina did. And now she's dead, thanks to your hell raisers."

There was no getting through to Jenna today. Obviously she had been traumatized beyond what Sera ever could have imagined. Sadness gripped her heart. *Vera would have known what to do.* She wished her mom's best friend had been spared a year ago.

"I don't have all the answers. But I understand how I feel in my heart. I'm the same person I was, Jenna."

Even as Sera said the words, she didn't believe them. She wasn't the same by any stretch of the imagination. She had committed murder, and if that wasn't proof enough she had changed, she didn't know what was. Yet her heart felt the same things it always had: anger, determination, but most of all, love. But CJ wouldn't be able to understand the distinction. CJ needed to see Sera as Serafina if Sera was ever going to get through to her old friend. But with demons on a mission to take over humanity, why should CJ trust her?

CJ stopped in her tracks, slowly walking toward Sera in deliberate and stable movements. When she was mere inches away, CJ glared at her. "I said my name is CJ."

She pulled a lighter out of her pocket. Sera jumped back. She wasn't sure if the lighter would work on her since she was an Ensoul. It was something no one knew, and neither Lorenzo nor Sera wanted to test the theory. Shocked at the lack of emotion from her best friend, Sera put her hands up.

"Okay, okay. I get it."

"Good." CJ's voice quivered as she spoke.

Sera wasn't sure if CJ sounded afraid or regretful of what she almost did. She hoped the latter. There needed to be a way to reach the girl she once knew, her Jenna, even if not now. When Sera looked up, CJ's team was right behind her, torches in hand. Sera backed away slowly. CJ seemed to notice because she waved them away until they made their way back to the bonfire.

"I didn't stay to upset you. I just wanted to talk," Sera said with a quiet, genuine sadness to her voice.

"There's nothing to discuss. You have your goals, and I have mine. Clearly we aren't on the same page. We aren't even the same species."

Sera couldn't argue with her. CJ was right on multiple

levels. The reality of Sera's new life and what it all meant began to come to light. It didn't sit well with Sera, not one iota.

"You're right. I was wrong to ask you to see it any other way. I should have known better. I'm sorry, CJ. I'm truly, truly sorry."

CJ's sharpness gave way to a softer expression before twisting back into the demon hunter leader she had become.

"Good. I'm glad we've agreed on something. Now, if you don't mind, I'd like to get back to my meeting."

"I'm sorry for interrupting."

"You're sorry for a lot of things." CJ began to walk away.

Sera called out, "And one more thing before you go."

CJ turned in Sera's direction, hands on hips as if annoyed. "Yes?"

Sera pulled her keys out of her pocket, took one of them off and tossed it into the air toward CJ.

CJ leaped to catch it. "Is this some kind of joke?"

"It's the key to Serafina's old house. She would have wanted you to have it."

Jenna had been having financial issues, according to Sera's research. Her best friend might have been avoiding her, but Sera cared enough to check up on her. Sera learned Jenna couldn't hold a job since her kidnapping, so she used Lorenzo's real estate access one day to discover Jenna's house was going into foreclosure. Soon enough, she would have nowhere to live. The two had drifted so far apart, Sera might never have seen Jenna again. Her noble former friend would have been mortified, now a prestigious leader in the new reality she created. Sera might have run into CJ hundreds of times, but would never have known it was her Jenna. CJ, the person Jenna had become, was nothing like her best friend.

CJ examined the key and looked up at Sera. She put it in her pocket and walked away.

Sera's heart sank. She had done the right thing, hadn't she? There was no way she would abandon Jenna now, not even under the tumultuous circumstances. Not even as CJ the demon hunter leader. All Sera could hope for now was that no one, especially not Lorenzo, would ever find out what she had just done.

CHAPTER 18

Damon abandoned Sera, leaving her with the red-haired demon hunter who looked a lot like the woman in Xander's video. He didn't want to believe it, of course, but he didn't have a choice.

Loyalty was the one attribute Lorenzo demanded from his leaders. Damon was his long-standing poster child. When Lorenzo led, all demons had better follow him. Had Damon stayed behind with Sera, it would have looked like he was disobeying his ruler's orders and he didn't trust Sera to handle the situation on his own. The latter wasn't true, and the former was a chance he couldn't take. At least not now.

Damon strolled up next to Xander on the sand. Damon's gut gnawed with the feeling something was going on between Xander and CJ. He figured he would see if Xander was honest and able to confide in him to start off. Xander had to have known the consequences of his actions if Lorenzo ever found out the truth about his demon hunter affair. Of course, Xander was allowed to have any inappropriate relationship on the planet, but demons needed to stay firmly planted on the side of demons. An affair with a demon hunter, especially CJ, would not bode well with their ruler.

Even more disturbing, CJ wasn't to be trusted, which meant Xander might not be either. Formerly Sera's best friend, Jenna, she had been the rock Sera had needed all of her human life. Damon hadn't known CJ well when she was Jenna. He had known what she meant to Serafina back then. Sera risked her life for the girl who was like a sister to her and the only true friend she ever had. Now they were both entirely different people and the past was light years away.

"Dude." Xander grinned. "What was that all about?"

"Lorenzo's way of dividing us, making it known to the enemy a war is approaching. Sneak attacks aren't his way, you know that. He needed to let the demon hunters know, with unequivocal certainty, a fight for their lives has begun."

"Makes sense." Xander shrugged, not having anything of substance to add.

Damon was about to ask Xander about CJ when he felt a hand on his shoulder. Lorenzo seemed to appear in a flash beside them.

"I'll catch up with you later." Damon nodded to Xander.

Xander threw his hand up in acknowledgment and kept on walking.

Lorenzo pulled Damon close and whispered in his ear. "We need to talk immediately. In private."

"Yes, sir."

Lorenzo escorted Damon to Ocean Boulevard where Yohan waited with the car. "As it turns out, we need to put our plan in motion sooner than later."

"I'm ready."

Damon slipped into the stretch limousine as the rest of his peers scattered all over the beach for a relaxing day off. With Sera in the high-ranking position of Special Demon

Forces leader, his days off were nonexistent. In such a role, Mount Everest-sized expectations matched the risk.

"Good, because what I'm about to tell you will be shocking. Not only for you but for Sera."

Lorenzo pulled out the twenty-five-year-old whiskey and poured a few fingers into a tumbler for each of them, and handed one to Damon. Lorenzo had always liked his whiskey neat, exactly like his strategic plans. Damon sat up straight and took a sip. The whiskey lit his mouth on fire at first but then it went down smooth as butter. He closed his eyes for a moment, letting his shoulders relax. Alcohol helped, it always had.

"I can handle it. Shoot."

"I know you can. It's why we're here. In fact, you're the only person I can trust with information of any value these days. You're as loyal as they come, Damon. Even with the charade you pulled last year with Sera, you had her best interests at heart. If I had seen it at the time, maybe the struggles with my daughter wouldn't have existed back then. However, the important thing is we really do have the same goals."

Lorenzo took a few sips from his glass. Damon mirrored Lorenzo's actions.

"We do."

Damon was far from a loyal demon, then or now. He had been more than loyal once upon a time. He followed orders; it was his only way of life. He prided himself regarding his obedience. At least until he met Sera. She was human then and had done the impossible: stolen his heart in the blink of an eye. It was a heart he had never let feel anything at all. In truth, he didn't even realize it was possible for a being as evil as he had always been to feel anything other than negative emotions. Through Sera, Damon learned how open-minded demons experienced a full range of emotions if they found a way beneath the solid surface of pure anger and hatred living within. He had grown into the man he had always wanted to be through his love for Sera, and he would spend the rest of eternity thanking her with his loyalty.

"I'm pleased you agree."

Lorenzo was right. Damon had only challenged his ruler to protect the one and only woman he had ever loved. And it was the same reason he was willing to betray him this time around.

"I live to serve you," Damon addressed Lorenzo with an undeniable vehemence, even though it was a lie.

"Good. Then get ready because Sera isn't going to take the news I'm about to reveal to you well at all. We may lose her entirely. I need to be certain you're going to be on my side in the end, as you have always been. I'm not insinuating you betray my daughter. Rest assured, you're not aligning yourself with me because you don't love her but because you do. All you're doing in this war is for the greater good of our species, for all of demonkind. Sera will be emotional and irrational, even furious. She's not going to understand any of it because she'll refuse to believe CJ is not Jenna. Sera has lost so much already, and losing her best friend is something she's been unable to accept throughout her entire first year as a supernatural being. I've seen the look on her face when life goes on without her friend, and we both know Jenna is the one puzzle piece missing in her new supernatural world. Therefore, I suggest you choose your time carefully and wisely to relay the truth to her."

"You can count on me to do the right thing."

There wasn't a chance in hell Damon would stand by and allow anything happen to Sera. Furthermore, he would never turn his back on her even if Lorenzo demanded it for the greater good of demonkind. Damon had risked his life before for Sera, and he would do it again in a human heartbeat.

"CJ is more than a local demon hunter leader." Lorenzo

swirled the whiskey in his glass as he spoke, his legs crossed like a woman's. He was proper, cocky and as secretive as they came. Whatever he was about to tell Damon, it was only a thin layer of the truth he hid inside. Lorenzo never revealed it all—like a poker player with a full house, his face was as stoic as his cold heart.

"She's also a weak human who has several deep-rooted psychological issues."

"Indeed, and it's an understatement, but it's also not why we're here today. There's more to everything you think you know. Much more." Lorenzo took another sip of his drink as if to delay the truth a moment longer. His appetite for drama was something Damon never understood.

"Such as?"

The complex person CJ had become didn't surprise Damon at all. She had metamorphosed into something entirely different from her old self just as much as Sera had a year ago. Even though CJ had remained human. Her mind had changed as much as her appearance. She had become a far cry from the best friend Sera had once loved.

Lorenzo licked the whiskey off his lips. "The violence against you and Sera was strategically planned."

"I figured as much. The entire night seemed like it was choreographed more like a music video than an attack. Besides, we survived; that fact alone reveals an intention to induce fear, not death."

"For starters, you're right. However, it has more to do with the person who orchestrated your music video than anything."

It took a moment for it to register in Damon's mind, and then he sprang into his response. "I should be shocked, but I'm not."

The words didn't jive with how Damon felt. The blood percolated inside of his veins. If he allowed himself to feel all he wanted to feel, his fury would be uncontrollable. CJ would have no chance to survive, fire or no fire. Sera would never forgive him if he sought revenge on CJ without permission. As such, he needed to keep himself calm and steer clear of his brewing anger.

"No, Damon. You don't understand what I'm saying." Lorenzo placed his glass in the cupholder and leaned toward Damon, making it a point to capture his gaze.

Damon responded in kind. "I do. CJ is the one to blame for all of it."

Lorenzo said nothing at first, as Damon's words hung between them for a moment. "In more ways than you can imagine."

"She wanted revenge for Sera becoming a demon, which makes perfect sense. She sent her demon hunters after us to do her dirty work. Cowardly, but not surprising." Damon sipped his whiskey as he relaxed. The entire situation was disturbing for Sera but not a tragedy.

Lorenzo shook his head and sat back. "It's precisely as I've said, there's more to the story than what you think you know. CJ wasn't only behind the attack on both of you." Lorenzo paused a beat. "She was the demon hunter behind the bat."

When the realization of what Lorenzo had said came to the forefront of Damon's mind, all of his restraint evaporated into a cloud plume. His fingers wrapped comfortably around the thick, short glass and tightened in an instant. The tumbler snapped and cracked as shards of glass exploded in his palm.

Lorenzo didn't even flinch. In fact, his reaction was price-less. A smile spread from ear to ear, exposing his sparkling teeth. His eyes peered into Damon's. It looked as though Lorenzo urged him on.

Damon could feel the negative energy bellowing

throughout the empty space, growing by leaps and bounds as they drove along the shoreline. He was trapped in the confines of a moving vehicle, but if that had not been the case, he was certain he would have taken off running for CJ's Silver Lake cottage. He composed himself instead. If he ripped the girl to shreds, Sera would never forgive him. He had to play this one by the book. For the one and only time since he had met Sera, he was on Lorenzo's side.

Only now, Damon meant it with every fiber of his being. It was time to fight to the death, all for the woman he loved. No matter his past ties to the human race, Sera came before all of them. He would gladly give up his dreams and even his life for her as she had done for him.

"I'm all in."

CHAPTER 19

He's in. Lorenzo crossed his arms loosely in front of his chest and leaned back in the leather seat of the limousine. His main warrior was determined to fight with all he had, and that was everything to Lorenzo. "Now that's what I love to hear."

Damon's face contorted as if he was in pain. "I have a confession to make."

Excellent. Lorenzo eased up straight, dropping his hands into his lap. "You do?" He was ready to hear it all.

Damon shifted in his seat. "My quarterly report was incomplete."

Lorenzo rolled his eyes. "It's hardly a confession, Damon. It's not as though I'm going to fire you. We're on to bigger and better things now, wouldn't you say?"

"I would, but that's why I need to tell you exactly what I left out of my notes."

"All right. Suit yourself. What is it? Someone stealing from our petty cash fund? Is Owen sleeping with the receptionist? Gina has always worn whorish attire, so I wouldn't be surprised, but I, for one, don't mind at all. Otherwise, I can't imagine what it could be. But go on, tell me. Now you've got my boxers in a twist." Lorenzo leaned toward Damon.

"It's Xander."

"What has our diminishing-brain-celled friend gotten into now?" *Perfect, Damon. Keep going.*

"CJ."

Well-played, my friend. "Come again?"

"Xander is into CJ. Literally and figuratively. I saw them on the video. They were...together. I tried to confront him first to confirm, but I didn't get very far. I didn't want to wait any longer."

Lorenzo was a fantastic actor. Deceit was his middle name. He blinked several times. "CJ and Xander?" He laughed. "I don't believe it. Why would he want a scrawny and pitiful excuse for a human being when he has Hayden at his beck and call? CJ's not only weak, she's a coward in every meaning of the word. She's learned to hide behind her brute force meatheads, which is the only reason she has survived up until this point. I can't believe it." Lorenzo shook his head in forced denial.

Damon looked down. "It's true." His head shot up, and the rage in his demeanor returned. "Regardless of his reasons, you and I both know it is a major problem for all demons. He's not only a trust concern, but now Xander is a huge liability. CJ is a risk we don't want to take on right now. Any access she may gain to our motivations and plans could be catastrophic. She may not seem convincing on the surface, but she has plenty of insane and violent supporters under her little thumb. Some of them are not only passionate and vengeful, but they're also psychotic."

Lorenzo raised his eyebrows and pursed his lips, for Damon's sake. "You know I don't take betrayal lightly." He pressed the button for Yohan.

"Yes, sir."

"Take us to Xander..."

"Sir, if you don't mind me interjecting. I have an alternative solution."

Lorenzo looked to Damon and then directed Yohan. "Hold."

Yohan turned off the intercom, understanding Lorenzo's command.

Lorenzo sneered at Damon. "Let's hear it."

"We need Xander."

"If everything you told me is true, I disagree. We don't need someone we don't trust."

"Normally, we don't. However, if Xander has insider access to the demon hunters' world, we want to keep him close to us. If I'm wrong and he betrays us anyway, I'm willing to pay the full consequences."

"You're not wrong. If you thought for a millisecond you were wrong, you never would've spoken up. You know better than anyone how I handle such betrayal. The details you've shared with me about one of my trusted leaders are a deal breaker. A life ender." The gravity of his message was more for Damon's ears than anything. Lorenzo always played the part.

"Even so, we should give him an opportunity to prove himself to us—to you. I can't imagine if given a choice Xander would choose a human, especially one that's a demon hunter, over preserving his own existence."

Lorenzo pretended he considered Damon's words. He wanted the battle between them to get as dramatic as possible. It would only cement his position, further drawing Sera to his side. More importantly, he had a duty to keep everyone under his control at this point when the world was about to explode in war.

"If I'm not satisfied with the outcome, I will take matters into my own hands. Do you understand?"

Damon nodded. "Loud and clear."

"As far as CJ goes, how do you plan to handle her involvement?"

"We both know Sera's going to want to handle this issue."

Lorenzo clapped his hands together. "Fine. I trust the two of you will deal with this immediately? Of course, you can ask for assistance if needed. I'm more than happy to lending a helping claw."

"Given the betrayal Sera will feel, I don't think any help will be necessary. CJ isn't going to have anywhere to hide. No demon, including Xander, will be able to save her."

"We don't have a lot of time. Xander and CJ are small peanuts compared to what's next on our agenda." Lorenzo pressed the intercom. "Take us to the bunkers." Lorenzo poured a brand new glass of whiskey and handed it to Damon.

Damon scrunched his face in confusion. "Bunkers?" Damon slid back in his seat and sipped his fresh drink. He would need it for what he was about to see.

"Damon, my son, you're about to embark on a brand new understanding of the human race."

YOHAN PULLED THROUGH THE GATES AT BARNACLE BAY, the peninsula at the north end of the Jersey Shore along Maroon County. Sandwiched between the ocean and the bay yet secluded from the mainstream beachgoers, Barnacle Bay was the perfect place for an underground hideaway. The limousine shook as it drove over the sandy and pebbled roadway. The sunlight reflecting off of the ocean peered through the slit in the tinted window Lorenzo had opened. There wasn't a soul in sight.

After a few more miles of driving in silence, Lorenzo

spoke. "It's not safe for us to be here. Not even with our powers. There are typically demon hunters on guard, and we'll need to be able to control large groups with ease." Lorenzo pulled out two containers from his suit jacket. "First, we'll need these for strength."

"What are they?"

"The serum that metamorphoses us into super-demons and turns humans into jelly." He handed him a half vial. "Otherwise known as Blaze. This vial you'll drink right before we exit the car." Lorenzo handed over a weapon resembling a mini revolver.

"I've never needed to use a gun in my life, not even as a cop." Damon eyed the steel weapon.

"Well, it isn't your typical firearm. It's filled with Blaze, the same as what you're about to drink. I realize it may seem antiquated, but you'd be surprised at how every human being reacts to the sight of a gun. Even if for a split second, it will make them pause. It's all we need to control a situation liable to get out of hand fast." Lorenzo showed him where the button, which wasn't a trigger at all, was located. "Press here and aim in the general direction of your target. You'll have the precision of a sniper—you can't miss—with the blast of a shotgun, far and wide."

Damon examined the small weapon in his hand. He looked unsure what to make of it but slid it in his pocket anyway. "If you say so."

Lorenzo smiled. "We're here."

Yohan turned off the engine, got out of the car, and opened the door for them.

"Ready?" Lorenzo tilted his head in the direction they were headed.

"As I'll ever be."

They clinked the vials together and drank the Blaze.

Lorenzo experienced the surge immediately. Damon had too because he watched him stretch and flex with the high. Lorenzo could tell Damon embraced the energy he had absorbed from the super serum.

"What do you think?" Lorenzo threw his palms up.

"Unreal." Damon examined his body. "I feel like I could fly."

"I've never tried it, but I wouldn't be surprised if we could." Lorenzo chuckled.

Once they were on the sand, Lorenzo waved Yohan away. "He needs to disappear. You never know who could be watching. A limousine draws a lot of attention. He'll be back in a half hour to check on us."

Damon shrugged. "I'm not concerned." He took off running to the ocean in a blur and skidded to a stop right before the wave washing ashore reached him. In an instant, he spun around and hightailed it back to where Lorenzo stood waiting. He was clearly testing out the Blaze, getting a sense of the insane amount of power within him.

Lorenzo had been getting his system accustomed to the powerful elixir for months, so his reaction was more controlled each time he ingested the extra energy. With Damon, on the other hand, it was a new experience and only natural for him to let off some physical steam.

It was good. Lorenzo would need Damon in control of himself when under the influence in coming days.

Damon roared like a lion as he arched his back.

"Better?" Lorenzo raised his eyebrows.

"Getting there."

"Good. Let's go." Lorenzo led them through the sand into an unkempt area of the beach where tall weeds grew and dunes formed. It was as though they were walking deep in the forest versus a sandy oasis on the east coast.

When they reached the place where the ground opened up beneath them, Lorenzo stopped short. "Here we are."

Damon looked around, confused. "In the middle of nowhere? I don't see a thing."

"Of course you don't. Humans never want us to see what's right in front of our faces."

Lorenzo took a few steps to the right and invited Damon along with a wave. They were no longer standing on pliable sand. It was as though the ground had been replaced with metal flooring.

Damon stomped his foot. "Damn it, if you're not always right."

"I set out to find the truth, and if I'm right along the way, it's a bonus for all of us." Lorenzo backed up, fanning out his hands with drama. "My son, you shall do the honors."

Lorenzo knew it would be better if Damon went through the process of uncovering the bunkers all on his own. He wanted Damon to remember how the metal felt on his fingertips and what the dark hole deep into the ground looked like from above so when he told Sera the news there was emotion in his story. Damon got on his hands and knees in broad daylight. He used his forearms to move the piles of sand around, shifting it off of the opening and onto the actual beach nearby. In no time it was uncovered completely.

"It's off the beaten path but not completely hidden. Dare I say those humans can be as devious as demons?"

"You're not kidding."

Lorenzo knew the latch was not visible. The only means to open the door to the underground was a scooped lever embedded in the door itself. He leaned in to watch as Damon found it, grabbed hold of it, and lifted it up and away from the ground. Damon wasted no time, the Blaze likely helping him along.

"I'm going in." In his next breath, he lowered himself into

the hole in the ground until his feet hit the ladder rung beneath him.

"Right behind you." Lorenzo quickly fell in step behind Damon. He immersed himself in the blackened underground prison.

It was time to prepare for a world war.

Rafaela cozied up to her husband, who held her close. She was loved, and her daughter would be loved, and that was all that mattered in the world.

"Some decaf tea, darling?"

"Yes, dear. Thank you."

Rafaela pulled the blanket up and readjusted herself on the couch. So much had changed, and she could hardly remember the person she used to be before Lorenzo came into her world. Since then, her life had taken a nosedive, resurfaced and turned itself inside out and upside down again. And right when she was about to lose her sanity, she found a sprinkle of hope in the form of an honest-to-God angel.

Her husband, Michael was a decent man in every sense of the word. He was caring, stable and, most importantly, he understood her plight in life. Many loved him, which, in Rafaela's opinion, was the measure of a good man.

Rafaela had been entirely wrong about things before. Letting her heart lead and her head fall apart was not the smartest of strategies in life. Lust with Lorenzo paraded itself as love, and that kind of deceit was the most dangerous emotion of all. It lied to her, making her believe what she had was real. Like a drug, it seduced her until she would have done anything to get another hit. Before long, she crashed and burned like every other addict.

Lorenzo had been the perfect drug for Rafaela. He was gorgeous, passionate, successful and also highly untouchable. The exclusivity about him was what drew her in, kiss by insatiable kiss. In the end, he was the devil in an Ivy League suit: a wealthy bad boy who, in many ways, ruled the world.

He was the man who took risks, walking the tightrope of life, teetering but always regaining his balance. He carried her with him until she felt truly safe, even though the fall from the top was deadly.

She had thought the fact that he was different from other demons was a blessing. For one, his eyes were brown, not the opalescent white like all the other demons. And at other times, they were blue or even green. When Rafaela confronted him, Lorenzo had told her they were color contacts. It made sense since a lot of demons were using color contacts to hide their identity. It was nothing new. Up close, she had taken notice of his eyes and there were no contact lines. There was no difference in the depth of his irises. No matter how much she wanted to believe him, Lorenzo didn't look like he wore contacts at all. His irises looked like they simply changed colors from day to day. She didn't know how it was possible, but for such a benign fact, it didn't matter to her. Who cared if he had blue or brown eyes? Not Rafaela.

"Here you go, love." Michael handed Rafaela the tea and went back to fixing dinner.

She took a sip, gazed into the fire and a surge of peace for her life as it was at that moment rushed her. Not so long ago Vera had told her a truth that changed everything.

Lorenzo wasn't an average demon. He was a special kind

of demon called an Ensoul. As far as Vera said she knew, Lorenzo was the only one of his kind. She had never known another Ensoul before. Of course, there were a lot of unknowns with Lorenzo because of his identity. None of them made Rafaela comfortable since there were so many uncertainties as to what he was or what their child would be.

Vera revealed Lorenzo wasn't only an Ensoul but the most powerful supernatural being on the Earth—the one and only ruler of all demons. Armed with the new knowledge, there was only one choice for Rafaela. She was a mother now, and it forced her to move away from the madness that was Lorenzo.

As it turned out, Lorenzo took it well. He didn't argue with Rafaela. He didn't even put up a fight. Instead, he respected her wishes—with a catch. Serafina would live her life as a human being without any interference from Lorenzo, or any other demon for that matter, until she turned twenty-five years old. At that time, the truth of her heritage would be revealed.

Rafaela's heart panged; Lorenzo had broken it that day. She knew then it was over. She would never forgive him for what he had kept from her. The depth of his dishonesty was too heavy a burden to bear.

Rafaela stroked the angel around her neck, the one meant to protect her. It was the only remnant left from Lorenzo, one with which she would never part.

The flames crackled and spit as Sera put another log on the fire. It was an unusually frigid night for September in New Jersey, one more like January. While the old mansion was built to last, holding its heat like a wood burning stove, Sera couldn't shake the chill inside of her bones. Curled up in a ball on the oversized leather couch, Hope howled for the one who saved her.

"Coming, pup. I'm making it a nice warm night for us."

Hope rolled over, pressing her back deep in to the cushions and twisted around. Sera fell onto the couch next to her, scratching the dog's belly.

"Oh, you're such a good girl. Such a good dog."

Sera gave her one last rub and shifted into the corner of the sectional up against her pup. She pulled a plush faux fur blanket over both of them. Hope squeezed into the space between her owner and the couch, perfectly content to be cuddling with a demon.

Finally, able to exhale, Sera grabbed her glass of Pinot Noir on the end table beside her and took a long, drawn-out sip. The fireplace mesmerized her. Ironic that a demon like

Damon would have such a contraption in his house. Fire was the only element able to remove him from the earth forever. She hadn't tested the same theory on herself as an Ensoul. As far as she knew, she could die by the same flame as any other demon.

Sera supposed it wasn't as uncommon as one would think for demons to have fireplaces, candles or gas stoves. Humans had been living with deadly objects in their lives since the beginning of time. From the cars they drove to the medication in their cabinets and even fireplaces in their homes, too. Most of the time, though, humans never realized how something so simple could be the one thing that took their lives away from them. At least with fire, demons were well aware of the consequences it threatened. Sera closed her eyes to push the horrid day behind her and find a calm place.

The front door flew open. Damon burst her relaxation bubble. He slammed the door behind him.

"We should talk."

Sera sat up straight. "Talking is overrated. Can't you see I'm trying to relax here?"

She was half joking but truly desperate for one evening without any worries or conflict. Unfortunately, it didn't look like it was going to be that kind of night.

Damon stormed toward her on the couch. "Let me rephrase. We need to talk."

She could practically touch the boundless energy seeping from his pores. His oversized pupils almost completely blocked his opalescent irises. Sera shifted, pushing back until she sat upright. Hope responded in kind, hunching her back and pulling her legs in close. Even the dog knew something in Damon was off. She began whining.

"What's wrong with you?" Sera never stopped stroking Hope as she confronted Damon. The dog calmed her in more ways than she would ever have imagined. Hope didn't only lower her blood pressure; she was her sedative with dog hair. The reality hit her—hard.

"We don't have much time," Damon said.

"What did Lorenzo do to you?"

Damon paced around the living room in circles. "The demon hunters are on a deadly mission. They're after all of us."

Sera slammed her wine glass on the coffee table. "He gave you the elixir. The Blaze. Bastard."

"It's worse than anything I've ever seen. We need to take action. And now."

She shook her head in disgust. "Your fierce determination. The devil in your eyes. He drugged you, too."

"What are you talking about?"

Damon's eyes were wild. She had never seen him like this before. Sera squinted at him in confusion.

"You didn't take anything from Lorenzo? A serum? A pill? He gave you Blaze. I know it."

Damon's face relaxed. "He did...but he didn't drug me. It was to prepare me, to prepare *us* for the impending war."

"Sure, that's what he wants you to believe. All of a sudden you're one hundred percent on his side. Doesn't that seem odd to you?"

She cocked her head, waiting for his response and hoping he would catch on to her insinuation. Damon moved closer, looming over Sera. His voice was as deep as a sonic boom.

"I don't have time for this. I need you to listen to me."

Sera flew up from the couch to face him. "Don't you dare threaten me, Damon Serpe. I'll listen when I'm ready to listen. You should know by now that I don't take orders from you. I'm not listening to anything you have to say in your condescending tone."

Damon took a few steps back, obviously realizing his

misstep. He softened his posture and his voice. "I'm sorry. I didn't mean..."

Sera put her hand up. "It's the Blaze. I get it." She patted the couch next to her. "Sit." Sera had done her share of flying off the handle when she was human. Surprisingly, as a demon, she had better control of her emotions. "Tell me what's going on."

Damon's body visibly relaxed, even if it was a tedious chore to get it into that state. The way he held himself in place on the couch told her the Blaze still raced like wild horses through his veins. He wanted to take off, she could tell, running toward whatever had shaken him.

"Lorenzo took me there. To the bunkers. They're right in the middle of the beach, can you believe it?" His voice trailed off as if he asked himself the question.

"Bunkers? It's not 1965, Damon."

"It might as well be. We're at war, only it's not overseas this time." The pace of his voice sped up. "You should've seen them. Dark. Desolate. Cold. It was hell on earth down there. We were underground."

"Underground? At the beach?" Sera had recalled hearing about private underground hideaways demons built along the shoreline, but never humans. Apparently, they had caught on to the value of secrecy, especially when dealing with a race of exceedingly powerful beings.

Damon didn't miss a beat; he kept fast-talking as if it were a contest.

"Prison cells. Solid as anything I'd ever seen. Even on Blaze, bending them was near impossible. It could be done, but no demon should even bother trying without power-enhancing drugs. It was as if the bars were supernatural themselves. It's impossible since humans built them."

"I know I'm new to all of this, but I've never known a demon who didn't try everything and anything, no matter how brutal, to survive. They don't exactly have a moral code."

"Fire's enough of a moral code. These hunters thought of everything. Like a sprinkler system, there are pinholes everywhere—from the floor to the walls to the ceiling—all connected to a complex system of gas piping. The flick of a switch or turn of a dial is all that's needed to set us all on fire. I can't imagine what demons will do when they are trapped with no escape."

"Maybe I missed something. Does mind control no longer work? Can't they use sheer will to make the humans unlock the doors?"

"In theory, it would take a lot of power to control a group of humans. And from what Lorenzo understands, the humans in charge won't even be visible to demons trapped in cells. They'll be controlling everything from an undisclosed location. The technological advancements make this an entirely new war on demons, a silent one. Humans who can wirelessly control our fate are hazardous to a degree we haven't experienced yet."

Sera let his story simmer in her mind. Whose side was she on anymore? She had no idea. It wasn't acceptable for humans who preached equality to suddenly change course and allow these obviously psychotic hunters to take over the world. They were no better than the rogue demons who slaughtered innocent people on a whim.

The storm inside of her was growing. Damon was right. She would have to take action. And soon.

"We can't let this happen. It's wrong on all levels."

Sera's heart began to beat faster. Her mood changed, and she didn't like it, but it was necessary. It was survival.

Beware of the truth.

Sera's mother's words came back with a vengeance. The truth was ever-changing and never-ending.

"We do." Damon's expression tightened. "There's more to it."

"What's the plan? Did Lorenzo give you instructions?"

Sera was surprised at how her direction had changed course so quickly. She had gone from calm and subdued into fight mode in a matter of seconds. Living life on the edge had an effect on her. Lately, it was the only way for her to live. Hope's ears perked up. She was on high alert too.

"Blaze is our plan."

"You and I both know drugging demons isn't going to solve anything."

It was the same old story. Lorenzo didn't want to solve the problem. He wanted to use brute force to eliminate his woes. It was one thing to experiment on her—she had asked for this crazy life. But to subject all of his people to a fate without any say in their own lives would only infuriate them. Added to their uncontrollable superpowers, the humans would have no chance whatsoever of survival. Mass murder wasn't the answer no matter who was killed.

"Not just demons, Sera."

Sera digested his words. She understood it all now. Clear as day. She stood up abruptly.

"I don't condone any of this. Not even a little. I never wanted to harm humans. That's not going to change because Lorenzo says it's what we need to do."

Damon placed a hand on her shoulder. "It's not so simple. They're going to kill us. All of us. Do you understand what I'm saying?"

"There has to be another way."

"I wish there was. But you didn't see what I saw tonight. It might as well be a medieval torture chamber in those bunkers. Once the hunters capture us, and they will, there's no way for us to escape. Blaze is our only hope. As an offense and defense."

"I'm sorry, this isn't football. This is our life. And those innocent people's lives." Sera stood, now looming over Damon. "Let me guess. Lorenzo has plans to give all of his demons the Blaze, his own concoction, which will ignite their superpowers. He'll give it to all humans, transforming them into half zombies, so they fall under his complete control. What kind of war is he starting? Humans won't have any means of defense. Murder by drugging and being ripped to shreds. Honestly, it's not something I ever want to be around to see."

She began to walk away. Damon followed her.

"You're making a snap judgment here. You don't have all of the facts. We're already living in a war zone, only no one has had the courage to stand up and fight for us. No one has admitted that what went on all of those years ago is happening again. Worse now. Demon hunters are taking over. They're torturing us. Turning on their friends and family who associate with demons. They're becoming the evil they say we are. Does any of this resonate with you?"

Sera snapped her head around. "Resonate? Yes, it resonates with me. I'm sorry, but maybe you've forgotten. A year has passed too quickly, hasn't it?" She couldn't help her sarcastic and accusatory tone. "I had to murder one of my best friends to save the other one. The psychotic demon friend who, by the way, I've turned into. Now my lifelong childhood friend, who's practically a sister to me, won't even look me in the eyes. How do you think it makes me feel?"

Damon reached for her, but she stepped backward. "I didn't mean..."

"To upset me? No, you didn't. I know this sounds like I'm taking it all out on you, but the fact of the matter is I'm sick and tired of Lorenzo falling back on the notion of all demons becoming extinct tomorrow if we don't do something horrific to the human race. It's an excuse. It's a cowardly and narcissistic cop-out. We are the evil, Damon. We are the terrible and horrendous race wandering the earth. And listening to you has made it crystal clear to me that I'm one hundred percent accurate in my thinking. I'm so quick to accept who I am now because I made myself into this horrendous evil. I did this. And the last thing I want to admit is that I killed my human self in error. Of course, I want to feel righteous about my supernatural life, but the reality is...I'm the epitome of failure. I've let down the one and only human being who loved me and believed in me exactly the way I was, flaws and all. Now look at me. I'm a devil in disguise. I know for certain my mother and father didn't want me to become this evil monster. I chose the evil path in life. I'm nothing more than a vicious murderer."

Damon's face fell. He took a few steps back. "I had no idea you felt so strongly about us."

Sera's words had sliced him open as if she had taken a machete to his gut. She had reflected her opinions right back onto him as if he were the devil and all of the evil in the world combined. Her heart dropped like a brick. She wanted to take her words back, sucking in the emotions they gave birth to, before the one good thing in her life was as damaged as she had become.

She stepped toward him. "It's not you. It's me. It sounds cliché, but I'm struggling with my identity and whom I'm supposed to be protecting. I was human once. Whether I want to admit it or not, it still impacts every single choice I make. I can't forget how to be human, even if most of my humanity is gone now. We both know there's a thread of it weaving its way through my heart. I can't cut the string, Damon. I don't want to cut it."

Damon got closer, wrapping his arms around Sera. She fell into him. Life was damn hard. She had done it all to herself. She pulled away from him and turned to the stairs.

"I need a minute to collect myself."

Hope jumped off the couch to follow her upstairs. Damon took deliberate steps behind her.

"We don't have a lot of time. The last thing I want to do is to pressure you into taking action, but there's more to the story. You haven't heard it all."

About halfway up the stairs, she turned to face him.

"I transformed into an Ensoul to save humanity, not to destroy it. If my life is in danger, then so be it. I signed up for this, no one else. Nothing you say will make me feel differently."

"It was CJ," Damon roared.

Sera spun around. "Excuse me?"

"The demon hunter with the bat and the person who commissioned those bunkers are the same exact person. It was CJ. Formerly your Jenna."

No. Not Jenna. Jenna had almost killed her. She was no better than Alison.

Sera shook her head vigorously in disbelief. "No. No. No."

"I'm sorry." Damon dropped his head in shame.

The best friend Sera had saved, the woman who refused she was Jenna and who had a key to Sera's old house, wanted her dead. It couldn't be true.

Beware of the truth.

She didn't want to believe any of it, but no matter what performance enhancing drugs Damon was on, he would never be so cruel as to lie to her about something so heartbreaking. If Jenna could turn on her like Damon had said, so maliciously, then the world and everything she understood about it had changed beyond her recognition. It wasn't anything like it had been a year ago. Nothing was the same, nor would it ever be again.

Sera swallowed the good intentions that had brought her to the supernatural side.

Humanity wasn't only a distant memory. It was a foreign language Sera could not comprehend.

She stood tall, even with the weight on her heart dragging her down. "I understand."

She did. She understood all too well. She was going to have to fight for her life again, only this time it would be against the very person whose life she had saved. The only human she loved would become her only enemy. But before she did what she was asked to do, what she needed to do, and the one thing she couldn't have imagined doing a year ago, she would need to take matters into her own hands one last time.

With Hope following close behind, Sera made her way up the stairs. She had come so far, and now it was time to merge the kaleidoscope of conflicts in her heart. As her foot hit the landing where her best friend brutally beat her not so long ago, she made a vow she would never look back again.

CHAPTER 22

till your mind. Still your mind. Still your mind. CJ practiced patience, something she hadn't needed to ever do before.

The demon hunters she led relied on her fast-acting, problem-solving brain at all times, so she had become comfortable operating at a permanent fast pace. CJ was the no-holds-barred decision maker who jumped at a moment's notice to address the issues at hand, no matter how deadly. She was all for taking action and nothing more. Moving forward without emotion was all CJ cared about any longer. Merely sitting still was as catastrophic as dying in her mind. She had already died once. She wasn't going to let it happen again.

Jenna had been the opposite of CJ in every way possible. A sweet and sensitive girl who everyone loved but didn't respect. Everyone took advantage of Jenna, who would idly stand by and let it happen. She wore her heart on her sleeve. The same heart she often found broken into pieces by the people she loved the most. It was no surprise to Jenna that the people closest to her, Alison and Serafina, had done the most damage. Her former best friends had shredded her heart into slivers; although by different means, Alison and Serafina both had a hand in murdering Jenna. Now she was long gone.

CJ hadn't taken any pieces of the Southern-twanged goody two shoes along for her demon-hunting ride. A woman like CJ couldn't have a girl like Jenna pulling her down. Emotional baggage had no place in a world where CJ would be fighting for her life. Every single day. Her feelings and memories would not serve any purpose. Except to make her weak.

Weakness was a curse CJ had long broken.

The toaster popped her bread out. It was burnt, almost black, the way she loved it. The dark and dingy rye, hard as a rock, served as a reminder of her critical mission. She broke it in half, the singed toast exploding on impact, like the evil she would die to break. CJ crunched on her meal in time with the doorbell. There was no way Xander would be coming over for a rendezvous before noon, let alone at nine o'clock in the morning.

CJ headed for the hall closet. She reached in behind her lightweight fall coats to grab the fire thrower leaning against the wall. She strapped it over her button-down fleece pajamas.

She moved with stealth. CJ closed one eye to see out the peephole. A demon hunter she didn't recognize stood on her porch. Mirrored sunglasses reflected an image of CJ's front door, which was as beat up as she had been. She never did fix the door after Alison, her former best friend-turned-kidnapper-and-sadistic-murderer, had broken into her house that fateful night almost a year ago. The split wood and chipped paint told the story of why Jenna was dead and CJ had been born in her place.

CJ was a woman on a mission. She was proud.

She examined the woman hunter. There wasn't much to see. Most of her body was covered in black clothing, and she wore a baseball hat under a hooded sweatshirt that shaded what was exposed. The disguised person didn't want to be recognized. CJ wasn't sure if someone in hiding on her doorstep was good or bad news. Either way, she was prepared to fight, at least in her heart. If she were afraid of opening the door for one of her own, what would happen the day the demons came for her? And they would come for her. There was no doubt in her mind.

CJ unlatched the door and thrust it wide open. "Can I help you?"

The woman lifted her sunglasses for a brief instant. CJ immediately understood the disguise.

"I'm about to find out." Sera pushed past CJ and into the house.

CJ closed and locked the door behind Sera and followed her old friend into the kitchen. CJ pulled at her pajamas, embarrassed to be facing her old friend, now her enemy, in such a vulnerable state. But what could she do? Sera was bound to confront her sooner or later. They might as well get themselves on the same page. It was now or never.

"What are you doing here?"

Sera placed the sunglasses on the table and pulled out a chair. "Do you mind if I sit?"

CJ wasn't sure how to answer. "Fine."

She hurried around the room, closing the blinds and drawing in the curtains before any of her neighbors saw the enemy she harbored. Her old friend looked ten years younger and stunning on many levels. CJ wished she could go back in time and be her old self, Jenna, but it wasn't possible. Times had changed. CJ pointed the gun at her old friend. Being casual was no longer an option, pajamas or not.

Sera threw her hands up. "I'm not here for a fight. I just want to talk. Can we talk?"

CJ's arm shook. "I only have intelligent conversations with humans. Last time I checked, you're not human."

Sera laughed. "You got me there."

CJ lowered the firearm until it was level with Sera's eyes. "Don't use your mind control shit on me. I'll blow your head off. One press of a button and you're up in flames. Got it?"

"Got it." Sera flicked the hood off of her head and took off her baseball hat. "Please. Put the weapon down. You don't need it. I promise."

"You say that now, but I can't trust you." CJ's shaking slowed as her confidence rose.

"Don't you think I could have done something if I wanted to? I'm here to talk to you. That's all. Please relax."

It was true. Sera could have killed her already. CJ's anxiety was more a trust issue than fear. At least now she was in a mental and physical position to defend herself should something go awry. CJ reluctantly let the large weapon fall until it lay on its side, not far from her grip.

"Sit." Sera gestured.

"I'm not sitting. You can say what you need to say from there. I'll be right here." She chuckled. "I learned my lesson with you people. It's bad enough you're in my house. If anyone saw me talking to you..."

"I have no intention of any such thing happening. That's why I look the way I do. It's not for my protection but yours."

CJ considered her words. She supposed it couldn't hurt to hear Sera out. She did have a point. None of it meant CJ would let her guard down. She stood tall, staring her old friend down once again.

"What do you want from me?"

"The truth. Nothing more."

"The truth about what?"

"Your intentions when it comes to me. I need the truth to come directly from you. I've heard rumors, ones I don't want to believe. Unless you tell me a different truth, I honestly don't have any other choice but to believe. I know our relationship isn't the same. Things have changed a great deal between us. It's my one regret. The world around us has changed, too."

"Yours didn't have to change. Choosing evil was your choice. You have to deal with the consequences. Don't start complaining about it now."

"You're right." Sera looked away. "I only have myself to blame." Her eyes showed signs of the person CJ knew back when she was Jenna. "Before I take any steps forward, I need to know what I'm leaving behind."

"You know as well as I do you already left it behind."

Sera glanced away briefly as if CJ had struck a chord. "I'm here, aren't I?"

A pinch of reality hit her. Her heart sank. It wasn't Serafina. Sera was a demon. A lying, untrustworthy, evil, murderous demon was sitting at CJ's kitchen table. She needed to activate her anger...and fast.

CJ grasped the weapon leaning against her hip. Survival above all. She would never let her guard down around a demon.

"Ask your questions."

"Tell me the demons are wrong about you. Tell me you haven't turned into the heartless human being they say you are."

"Heartless? Aren't you the pot judging the kettle?"

"Be straight with me. Are you the one behind all of this, our war? Did you attack me?"

CJ wasn't sure how to answer the question. If Sera

attacked in response, she could kill her. "I'm only one person." CJ walked away toward the door.

Sera pushed the chair away from the table and stood. "Listen, I know you're different now. Hell, I'm miles apart from who I was, but none of it changed my heart. You're still Jenna to me, and I can't believe you'd ever do anything to hurt me. No matter what has traumatized you in your past. No matter anything."

Sera walked after CJ, who turned around to face her. She could feel the plethora of emotions bubbling to the surface.

Control yourself, damn it. Remember who you are. You're a demon hunter. This person in front of you is not who you think she is. She's a demon. She's a liar. She's evil. She'll take your head off when you're not looking.

CJ straightened and faced the demon. If she analyzed her gaze closely enough, she could see Alison in her eyes.

"You want to know the truth? Yes. It's me. I'm behind all of it. Every terrible wrong that has fallen upon your people lately is because of my direction and hatred for the demon race."

Surprisingly, Sera shook her head. "I'm sorry. I don't...I can't believe you. Jenna would never, *could* never flip a switch and become a person who hurts the ones she loved. She was vehemently against any violence. Clearly, CJ, you've been through a lot. But deep down inside, Jenna lives within you. Like Serafina lives within me. They made us who we are today. And while we're not exactly the same, we're not entirely different either."

Sera cracked a smile. It mocked CJ's transformation as if it wasn't as significant and life-changing as what Serafina had experienced. So what if CJ wasn't a different species? She was a different person. It had to count for something. No, Sera wasn't going to believe CJ until she showed her old friend the truth.

"Is that what you think?"

This time, CJ pushed past the demon. She reached far back into the closet and pulled out the proof. It was the truth Sera so desperately wanted, and CJ would give it to her straight this time. No words needed. When Sera turned around to face her, CJ whipped the bat up into the air. She held it above her head exactly as she did the same day she beat the demon ruthlessly.

"Does this look familiar?"

CJ watched as Sera's face filled with a surprising emotion. Not the usual rage she was used to seeing. Instead, it was pure, unadulterated sadness. Sera didn't say a word. She turned on her heels and left CJ's house.

And in one split second, CJ turned former best friends into brutal enemies, igniting a war with one wooden instrument.

When the door slammed, and Sera was gone, CJ wasn't expecting it, but she broke down into hysterical tears.

CHAPTER 23

Armed with more Blaze serum than any demon could fathom, Sera led an army of demon soldiers to the hunters' bunkers in the middle of the night. Damon led his own crew right behind her. Lorenzo had given them the arduous task of prepping their teams for battle.

They were ready for an all-out war.

They must know the enemy, Lorenzo had said. He had decided early on the bunkers weren't going to happen. Instead, he would lure the demon hunters there and turn things around on them without giving them a second to spare. Lorenzo would use the humans as bait. He would swap out the gas lines and pump Blaze in, creating a prison of their own making. Sera had to admit it was a brilliant strategy.

The old Sera would have had a problem with it. But the new Sera refused to question Lorenzo. In her loss of all hope for humanity, she had gained a sense of duty and obligation to her ruler father. He had known what was best all along. Questioning him had only set her back on her journey as an Ensoul.

One by one, the demons slipped underground. In the full

darkness, headlamps were the only light paving the way for the soldiers. It was their first time in the prison. If needed, they had enough Blaze on hand for each of them to use in the next twenty-four hours. With their powers exemplified, Sera and Damon had no worries at all. There was no way they could lose.

Their mission was all about survival of the demon species. Sera was willing to fight to kill anyone who tried to take her, or Damon, down. Or any of her demon brothers and sisters for that matter. Notwithstanding what she thought was right or wrong anymore because there was no such thing as right or wrong. The lines had blurred too much for moral codes to be defined. The decent remaining humans had turned evil. Jenna, now CJ, was her hardcore proof. Any demon who had tried to exemplify a human's version of good only proved demons were as deceitful as humans thought. It was a losing battle.

Sera knew better now. She was well aware of who she and Damon were deep inside. They may have been evil souls, but they had made a choice, one that challenged their willpower every single day. They had done it all for the sake of humanity because they respected those who were different from them. Unfortunately, the rest of the world wasn't on the same page. Humans and demons had been forcefully divided. World war was imminent. No shift in perspective would change a thing.

Once both of the elite teams entered the underground bunkers, Sera gathered them around for a quick team meeting. She moved around the space as she gave her speech.

"This is one of thousands of bunkers of its kind. Buried along shorelines all over the world, humans have built cages for us. Cages meant to trap, torture and kill our kind, thus extinguishing our species."

Groans speckled the crowd. Damon clapped to get the

demons' attention. The crowd hushed at the sharp sound. Sera waited for quiet and then continued.

"Tomorrow we go into battle with the human race. Demons all around the globe are on formal notice as of this moment. Lorenzo gave the word, and he wants to ensure it spreads like wildfire. Only this time, fire isn't our issue— demon hunters are, and they're why we're here and prepared to fight."

Euphoric bellows escaped the crowd as they pumped each other up with words of encouragement. Sera waited for the momentary celebration to end before speaking.

"In exchange for them trying to trap us, we're going to flip their world upside down. Their prison guards will become our prisoners. As Lorenzo has said many times before, our time to rule this world has finally come. We'll be in charge once again in the New World Regime. Only this time, there's no going back."

Roars of triumph echoed in the facility below the earth. Sera could feel her face beaming brightly. She was truly proud of her strength in such dark times, the same times responsible for previously making her question her loyalty. It had been a tumultuous ride. She was grateful to finally arrive as the elite Special Demon Forces leader she was always meant to be. Her sense of fulfillment had been worth every failure and triumph, the entire struggle. The faces of the followers staring back at her were not only driven to succeed but to do so under her rule. They respected her and treated her like they would have treated Lorenzo. She was flabbergasted at how quickly they had fallen under her command. She was certain Lorenzo was responsible. Sera made a mental note to thank him for all he had done for her after the bloodied sand settled.

"As you can see, we're split into two distinct and separate

groups. These are the elite teams Lorenzo organized for specific purposes in our crusade."

Damon shared the stage with Sera, backing her up on the orders she gave. He pointed to Sera's group.

"Sera's team is designed to secure the hunters. You're the Special Demon Forces Hunter Team and are expected to follow orders from Sera on how to successfully influence your demon leaders around the globe. There's enough of the Blaze serum to go around, so don't worry but also don't get greedy. Every demon on Earth will be amped up and ready to enter into battle. Once you have all of the demon hunters imprisoned, we will move into the second phase: subduing the general human public at large."

"Here, here," Sera said.

Damon addressed his team. "That's where my soldiers, Group B, come in. You're my Special Demon Forces Civilian Team. We don't want to attack with our guns blazing, as the human saying goes. We know there are more humans than demons on Earth right now. No amount of mind control is going to save our lives if humans collectively decide to move forward with their original plan and light the world on fire. Therefore, while Sera's team is rounding up the hunters in the dark hours of the night, we'll be rigging the waterways, infiltrating the airways and any other ways you can imagine to get Blaze directly into the bloodstreams and lungs of all humans left on Earth. And I mean *all* humans. Many of you have learned to fit in with humans nicely, suppressing your evil tendencies. Emotions such as empathy and compassion have inadvertently grown within you as well, an unwanted side effect of conforming to society. I know this first hand." Damon shot a glance at Sera, then back to his team. "While you may have the urge to kill, oftentimes your survival depends on finding a way to relate to and understand the human you're interacting with."

Sera stepped up next to him. "Damon is saying while you can't rip them all to shreds on a whim, you also need to forget all of the survival tactics you have learned about assimilating with the human population. It's a strategic balance. The Blaze serum will make it a difficult one to accomplish. It's precisely why the Special Demon Forces Civilian Team is comprised of the most well-adjusted demons. The ones who have learned when to hold back and when to press on. You have superior judgment, which is required for this task."

The Group B demons, including Hayden, lifted their chins a little higher, reveling in praise of their minds.

"However, make no mistake about it, you must use your brain wisely. Because in the end, you must refrain from exercising any sympathy or mercy. Understood?"

Sera made eye contact with several members of the group. The crowd cried out in cheers and roars.

Damon took over. "Settle down." He waited until they could hear him. "Contrary to what it sounds like, we're not out to merely kill every human in our sights. Our goal is to subdue them, which is a sizable difference. We must get the human crowds under control until we can transition into phase three, which is assimilation. More on that later, but for now, we want you all to have a clear understanding of what we're going to be doing in the next twenty-four hours."

Sera looked to her group. "While Damon's soldiers are mentally savvy, you're the most skilled fighters of all demons."

Xander beamed at Sera and her heart beat a little faster, hoping she could trust him in this most crucial hour. Sera squared off her stance.

"Your excellence in aggression and manipulation is the reason why you're on the Special Demon Forces Hunter Team, required to engage in the physical assault against the demon hunters. You're on the front lines and rightfully so.

Demon hunters are as brutal as they come. But they have no chance against any of you."

The Special Demon Forces Hunter Team bonded via exchanged roughhousing gestures all around. They were damn proud, Sera could tell. After the brutish confidence had waned, she continued.

"Our job is to capture all demon hunters in the dead of night, without any drama and without much bloodshed. You're to bring them to the underground bunkers nearest to your location in New Jersey. This is our designated area. In the rest of the country and around the globe, you are in charge of making direct contact with the local leaders Lorenzo has chosen to secure the hunters. You have all been given maps with their locations in the tablet included in your war packs. On your map, the demon hunters' homes are tagged in red, and the bunkers are labeled in blue. When you've accomplished your mission, you'll wait for confirmation of your leaders having done the same. Then, and only then, you will report back to me with a status update on your progress. Once I've given Lorenzo the green light that my Special Demon Forces Hunter Team has been successful, your objective will transition into statewide border control, as will the rest of your teams worldwide. You'll capture any hunters you may have missed to prevent them from sabotaging our plans. Next, Damon's Special Demon Forces Civilian Team will be able to take over operations without any unnecessary interruption."

Sera addressed the Special Demon Forces Civilian Team directly. "You'll follow Damon's orders and turn on the systems you'll have already ensured are ready to go, a task to be completed while my team rounds up hunters. By that point, you'll also have already infiltrated the water and air systems with Blaze. You'll have injected Blaze into the human food supply and into their medications. While there's enough of the synthetic Blaze to go around, you'll still want to use it wisely. We have a limited supply of pure Blaze serum, which is what the synthetic is derived from. The goal is to use the least amount possible so we have plenty remaining until we can get the world war under our complete control. Finally, we shall take our next-step orders from Lorenzo directly. Are there any questions?"

"How long will we have to infiltrate all of these systems? It's not an easy task." A demon with a bob cut and square black glasses peered down on Sera.

"Not long. A few hours."

There were a few grunts and complaints. "However, a few hours is plenty of time. Lorenzo has taken the liberty over the past year of preparing all of these systems. All you'll need to do is to connect with the demon at each plant and public facility designated by the project manager. They'll work with you on next steps so it all goes smoothly, which we fully anticipate. Again, these contact details are in your war pack."

Mumbles and sidebar conversations followed her explanation.

Sera crossed her arms, scanning the crowd. "Any other questions?"

"How much of the Blaze will we get?" someone else from the audience asked.

"Half of a vial of pure Blaze at a time for you to personally take. It's plenty to get by on, trust me. You'll also get an arsenal of weapons that use Blaze as their ammunition." Sera held up a messenger bag—the war pack—that carried all of the gear the demons would need. "Everything is in here. It's your war bag. I know what you're thinking, but don't try to drink the ammunition. It's diluted enough to subdue humans but will only be wasted on you. Like I said before, we need to conserve our supply."

"How can we get more?"

"When Lorenzo approves it."

Groans and murmurs from the crowd filled the air. "You'll need to go directly through Lorenzo's personal assistant, Gina. She's the one who is managing the supply. It's under strict watch and tight guidelines. As I said, we are taking this seriously and do not want to lose the one weapon we need the most."

Sera turned away to discourage more questions. "Anything else?"

"Yeah, I have one," a stocky demon near the front, who looked like he lifted weights, shouted out. "What will it do to us? Is it like demon steroids? The human performance enhancing shit won't work on us."

"In a way, yes. You'll have more strength and more power. You'll also heal almost immediately from any wounds you receive. And you'll be able to use mind control on many humans at once."

"What about fire? Can it still kill us?" a young female asked.

Sera thought it best to demonstrate. She gestured to Damon. Sera pulled out a lighter and flicked it on. Damon neared the flame. Gasps filled the room. He shoved his hand into the fire and pulled it back out.

"Voila." Sera grinned.

Damon raised his hand. It was temporarily red, then it disappeared and went back to its normal olive tone.

"Wow. So cool," someone from the group proclaimed.

Sera raised her hand to refocus their attention. "It's important to understand how Blaze works with fire. Flames won't kill you right away, that's true. But fire is still far from our friend. We aren't sure what exposure to flames in the long-term will do to us. We also aren't sure if there is a shelf life on the Blaze, meaning whether, after a certain number of hours beyond ingesting the serum, the fire protection wears off. What we do know is it protects us to a degree. But please, don't take any chances. I trust you'll make sure your risks are always wise choices. You must act as if your life depends on it because it does."

Sera put the lighter away. "Let's get into our teams and acquaint ourselves with the bunker space. While this is the main shelter at the Jersey Shore, there are many others in existence that look a lot like it. Some are set up differently, however. Since Damon and I haven't been to all of them, you'll each get an opportunity to understand the way they are laid out in your tablet of maps. Understand that in the end, it doesn't matter what shape or size they are. The most important part of this mission is to capture and subdue. You will figure it all out when you get there. I trust you will know what to do."

Damon threw the war packs out to the crowd. They caught them and strapped them on or passed them around. "Put them on but don't open them. We have to keep moving. You can go through the self-explanatory supplies Sera mentioned later."

Sera waved a hand behind her. "Follow me." She led the demon entourage through the bunker.

Damon spoke up. "Go ahead. Get inside. Become familiar with the cells. This is where your prisoners will live. You'll need to see things from their perspective if you want to know how to deal with them."

Sera directed the two Special Demon Forces teams to split up and use the next hour to examine the intricacies of the bunker, including the infusion system. She explained how the fumes from the Blaze elixir now replaced the gas and spark system. Lorenzo had completed the comprehensive shelter overhaul in record time given the threats on the horizon.

For the first time ever, Sera was truly proud to also call her ruler her biological father.

Damon put his arm around Sera, pulling her close. "You're a real leader, you know."

She waved him off. "Nonsense. I'm just doing my job. I made a choice to be here, so I'd better go all in, right?"

"You never do anything halfway." Damon kissed her cheek.

Sera shrugged. "What's the point?"

Damon looked away, deep in thought. "Balance. The yin and yang of life. Living to extremes never turns out the way you expect it will. The key is learning to balance the good with the bad, the right with the wrong; that makes everything fall into place the way it should."

Sera tilted her head up at him. "I'm not balanced?"

"You're driven. You'll find your own balance in time." Damon let go of her.

She tried to understand the meaning of his words, but there was no time. They were going to war. And right now, balance had no place in her life. Right now, she needed to take severe and deadly action.

"Let's head out," Sera yelled. One by one, her demon followers fell into place as she led them out from the underground bunkers and into the chilly, starry night.

CHAPTER 24

L orenzo sat at his marble desk in the Red Reef Enzo and Dell headquarters' office. He was adorned in his finest cloak embroidered with a twenty-four karat gold emblem of the coveted wings on fire, draped over an expensive suit and tie as if he were holding Supreme Court.

In many ways, he was.

The wings on fire icon shone as brightly as the sun, serving both as his backdrop and the default screen on the monitor raised high in the room. He hoped the symbol would be the catalyst to bond his demon viewers around the globe in their unified mission to extinguish the human rule.

"You're connected now." Owen handed Lorenzo a remote control. "Click this button when you're ready to turn on the live feed. The imaging is state of the art and three-dimensional. Your audience will see and hear you as if you were feet away from them in the flesh."

"Perfect." Lorenzo smiled.

Owen adjusted the clip on Lorenzo's neckline. "Your microphone will be muted until you begin the broadcast."

"Splendid. That will be all. I've got it from here."

Lorenzo waved Owen out of the room. Owen nodded and shuffled away, head down as always. Lorenzo trusted Owen with many company secrets; however, matters related to the demon race were shared with supernatural leaders only.

Lorenzo stopped Owen at the door. "Wait."

Owen turned on his heels. "Yes, sir?"

"Have Gina send them in. Cloaked." The next time Lorenzo spoke to Owen it would be in an entirely different kind of superior role.

"Will do." Owen left the demon ruler's office.

As Lorenzo waited, he recalled how the previous events of the day had panned out. He put Xander on notice to call off his business partnership with CJ, even though Lorenzo had been the one to order the relationship in the first place. Hayden was in the room when this was announced, of course. Lorenzo wanted to ensure both Xander and Hayden were on the same page and fighting for the same cause.

Xander had looked disappointed, although he had known from the beginning the affair would end at some point. Lorenzo assumed it was because Xander had fun messing around on the other side. Lorenzo could hardly blame him. Being in a relationship with a human was something he missed terribly since Rafaela had passed. Yet it was also the only decision he had made as an Ensoul that had weakened him. He didn't much care if Xander had an affinity for CJ or not. Lorenzo was, however, wildly concerned about Xander becoming weak as a result.

Weakness would not be tolerated.

Lorenzo had shared with them how his plans to disarm the demon hunters started with Xander and Hayden. Sera and Damon had taken care of surveillance on CJ's house, car and cell phone so they were aware of her whereabouts at all times. They would know immediately if Xander had betrayed

Lorenzo. Thus far, Owen had been charged with monitoring Xander, and while there was a lot of romance, no secrets were shared. With Xander's life at stake, Lorenzo didn't expect to be betrayed.

With the demon hunter leader under close watch, dismembering the rest of the hunters would be a simpler task. CJ may not have been a strong person, but she was a passionate leader when it came to using her mind. Her obsession coupled with the traumatic experiences with demons in her past had made her a force to be reckoned with, albeit a crazy one.

Crazy ran deep amongst the demon hunters. They might have had the guts to fight to the death for a cause, but they would never have made a move without CJ. She was the one with the story. Her life was the perfect basis for their mission. Before CJ, the demon hunters had been no more than angry humans without a purpose-driven life. They were looking for something to believe in, even if it belonged to someone else, and therefore, they were easily swayed to CJ's cause.

Emotions motivated everything one did, whether human or demon. Lorenzo excelled at guaranteeing only the strongest emotions were brought to light whenever he fabricated a war.

The door creaked open. Sera entered first, followed by Damon. The two elite Special Demon Forces leaders fell into chairs on either side of Lorenzo. They all faced the camera for the audience, proudly representing all of demonkind alongside their ruler.

Lorenzo glanced to the left and the right. Sera and Damon nodded, indicating they were prepared to proceed. He pressed the button to begin the live stream. A green light flashed, indicating they were broadcasting live on the Internet. He watched as the visual flashed from a flat photograph of the demon symbol to the on-air feed.

Serious faces stared back at them. Lorenzo was pleased with their appearance. They look like royalty, blank-faced and aristocratic, precisely as they should.

"Greetings from the Jersey Shore." Lorenzo spoke with a somber tone. "As you prepare for this evening's attack on humanity, I would like to remind you of the reason we're at this point in our existence, as well as offer you some words of encouragement." He cracked a shifty smile for a brief moment. "Twenty-five some odd years ago, I fell in love with a human being. Her name was Rafaela. As you can imagine, this isn't something I was prepared for as a super-natural creature. Evil beings don't fall in love, as I've often said. Certainly, I didn't think it was possible. That is until I found out I wasn't born as an ordinary demon. No, in fact, I was created as a rare and powerful demon called an Ensoul, and it's the reason I, and no one else, am your ruler."

Lorenzo raised his eyebrows and palms. "Now that I understand more about what being supernatural means, I can tell you some details about myself with certainty." He paused for effect. "I'm not much different than you are because I am, at the very core, still a demon. Yet, shockingly enough to me as I'm sure it is to you, I experienced the truest and purest of human emotions: love."

Lorenzo glanced at Sera and Damon, who had been prepped on the general theme of the discussion but not the details. Both were stone-faced and unreadable. Lorenzo was pleased.

"Why am I telling you about my love story instead of some pep talk about waging war on humans? Because, my dear demon friends, they're one in the same. You see, by falling in love with a human, I allowed myself to become vulnerable. I turned weak. In fact, so weak, that when I lost my dear, beloved Rafaela I didn't know what to do with the rest of my life. Dare, I say I almost took my own life as a result." Lorenzo looked down and away.

"Yet I found my inner strength. I summoned the genuine core of my being. In essence, I found my evil. And my evil, my demons, is what has saved me."

He flashed a knowing smile. "You see, from that moment on I learned that humans only had one purpose for demons in this world: to challenge us and to make us stronger. To understand them, to sympathize with them is to become weak like them. And as is the case with love, weakness never wins. The stronger party always takes the higher-level position in the relationship and the more vulnerable side always loses. In this case, we have assimilated to the point of becoming weak. And now, as in any relationship, the humans are enforcing their upper hand."

Lorenzo took a break to let his complex theories sink in. "You see, it wasn't Rafaela's fault at all. It was mine. And thankfully, I have no regrets. Sera is the result of our union and, well, I couldn't have asked for a better version of myself to have been brought into this world."

Lorenzo and Sera glanced at each other. She had no expression on her face.

"I'm only surmising, of course, what would have happened if Rafaela wasn't taken away from me so suddenly and at such a young age. But I can venture a guess I would have not gone down the path I've embarked upon today. I wouldn't be your fearless ruler. I'd more than likely be a suburban husband with a wife and child in tow, hiding who I was for the sake of all humanity."

Lorenzo shook his head in disgust. "I believe we're here for a reason. And unfortunately, Rafaela sacrificed her life for me in many ways. For that, I will always be grateful. But I can't forget the lesson her death taught me. Never deny your truest self, the demon you are inside. That, my friends, is what this world war is all about. We've been living in denial for so long that we've become human clones. For what reason? Look where it has gotten us. We've become target practice. Most sadly, our existence no longer has any meaning or value."

Lorenzo clenched his teeth, speaking in a confident and deliberate manner. "Tonight is when we shall take our lives back. Tonight, we'll become our truest selves. No one will be given the ability to weaken us ever again. Humanity won't hold us down, repressing who we are. We won't be stopped from living the way we were meant to live. We must embrace the parts of ourselves the world hates, those pieces we have been taught to deny about ourselves, and love the demon within each of us. We must embrace our evil."

After a moment, he shot a look at Sera to take it from there.

"In concert with my father's words, I support our mission tonight and every day and night after that. I promise to fight for you. I'll forever risk my life for you. I'd be honored to die for you. It's my vow to each of you, my fellow demons. You've been given a precious gift called life. Don't let anyone, human or otherwise, deny who you truly are. Don't let them try to take your existence away from you. If we don't believe in ourselves, who will believe in us? I'm here to say I believe in myself. And I believe in you."

Damon picked up where Sera left off. "You're strong, and you will survive. We have taken the necessary measures to ensure it. Trust in your leaders and have faith in yourself. We're behind you one thousand percent. Like Lorenzo and Sera said, we are all unique beings, and we are here for a reason. It's time to take our lives back, to take our world back and to do it with grace and purpose."

Lorenzo smiled at his protégés and concluded. "Now that we've spent enough time on the verbosity, I'd like to end this broadcast with one last thought. Your life is worth something. I expect you to fight to the bloody death to survive. Don't let me down. So I'll end by saying something at the core of our existence. My final and perpetual advice to you: always embrace your inner demon."

He let the image of the three of them linger briefly before hitting the off button. The screen faded to black. Gina came into the room to disassemble the equipment, receiving the cue they had rehearsed. From the corner of his eye, Lorenzo noted the signal. She had done exactly as he had asked. Owen lay slumped in her chair behind the front desk.

Lorenzo's heart thumped in time with the theme music ending their show.

It was official. The war had begun.

CHAPTER 25

CJ sat on the edge of her kitchen chair, and her sanity. Alex had not returned her call all day. She had no idea where the hell he was. It wasn't about the sex or the emotions attached to the sex any longer. It was all about his safety—and hers.

Alex knew it was the eve of the attack. Maybe he was back to acting as Xander, the demon, and not Alex, her boyfriend. Perhaps he had revealed everything she had shared in confidence with him to Lorenzo. It was more possible than she cared to admit. Maybe she couldn't trust him after all.

CJ ripped a cuticle off with her teeth and yelled aloud. Blood trickled at first and then poured from the open wound on her finger. She rushed to the sink and put her thumb under the faucet. Cold water flushed the blood away, turning the water pink. She applied pressure to it with a napkin to stop the bleeding.

Who was she kidding? Nothing was okay. It never would be again. She was likely going to die tomorrow. And for what? To prove she was a decent person? She was the best kind of person that ever existed.

Despite losing her best friend and now her lover, there were still hundreds of people backing her up. They were willing to die for her. They risked their lives for her on a daily basis. Not many people could say such a thing with certainty.

CJ smiled at the thought, which soon fell with her heart when she opened her email. She replied to everyone on the message she had sent two days ago to her team. The only people who she could rely upon in such dire times.

Date: Saturday, September 6

Time: 11:45 p.m.

Subject: Re: URGENT - UPDATE

In a few short hours, we'll set the world on fire. I wanted to take this opportunity to thank you for all you've done for me, each and every one of you. After tomorrow, you won't be demon hunters any longer; you'll be global heroes. Humanity is blessed to have you. Godspeed, my friends.

--CJ

After sending the email, she checked her messages. There were no texts and no calls. Nothing from Alex. Why hadn't he contacted her? She dialed his number one more time. His voicemail answered. She hung up. CJ wished it were twenty years ago and she could slam the phone down. Simply pressing *end* on her cell was anti-climactic.

Damn him to hell. The thought was truer than she could ever have imagined.

CJ pulled her hair back. She slipped on one of her basic black hats, then grabbed the keys to her beat-up truck. She loved her truck. Trading in Jenna's suburbia-style Japanese sedan for an American made 4WD had come in handy. It had also proved to be one of the best decisions she had made in the past year. Demon hunting notwithstanding.

After securing her house, she took off to locate Alex. She would find him if it were the last thing she ever did. She had a feeling it might be.

She didn't have to go far at all. In fact, only two miles from her home. While parked under a light by the beach, she saw them arm in arm walking out of CJ's favorite bar. Hayden and her boyfriend, Xander, were too close for comfort.

CJ's lover, Alex, was nowhere to be found.

She bit her bottom lip hard. *That bastard.* Could she blame Alex though? He did have to keep up appearances. As selfish as it was, on the night before everything went up in flames, she wanted him by her side. Not attached to Hayden's hip.

CJ punched her leg in frustration. Jealous thoughts bounced around in the cage of her mind. She could barely concentrate. She didn't know what to believe anymore. Everything was coming to a head. All she had worked for was about to pay off. She should be happy. She should be damn thrilled about it. Instead, she was shattered inside.

When the light turned green, she sped down the nearest side street. She parked alongside the curb and turned off her headlights. CJ sat silently in the dark where she made an executive decision.

She would stalk her lover and his girlfriend.

CJ shouldn't have been surprised at what Alex was doing. It was exactly what demons did well. They lied. They made people crazy with barely the blink of an eye. Still, she couldn't help herself. She wanted him in every way possible. There was something innate in her desire to be under his control. Little could be done to expel it. No matter how wrong he was for her, her heart knew otherwise.

The demon couple strolled to his convertible. He opened the door for Hayden. CJ was nauseous. Even if it was an act, it killed her to watch them. She had always known about Hayden, but CJ had never seen them together. Especially not when she was as vulnerable as she was tonight. The significance of the future events highlighted everything.

When Hayden's door was shut, Alex made his way to the

driver's side. His head turned in her direction, and for an instant, CJ swore Alex saw her there in the car. A slight smile crossed his face. She wasn't sure whether to find comfort in the little sign, if it was a sign at all, or furious at showing off his gorgeous girlfriend to her. If CJ hadn't been in love with him, she would have thought Xander and Hayden made the better couple. They were both terribly good looking and the same species, which helped in wartime. CJ couldn't let what she was seeing in front of her face skew her reality. Alex was the man underneath Xander's façade.

Alex belonged to her.

Nothing about him being with Hayden was right. It was all wrong. As the sports car flew down Ocean Boulevard, CJ started her truck and pulled out slowly behind Alex. His car was hard to miss. A shocking red, top-of-the-line race car he drove with the top down year round.

CJ took her time following him, knowing she couldn't lose him. If she couldn't see him, she could hear him from a mile away. The low, throaty growl of his engine was enhanced tenfold due to a turbo booster. It sounded like the king of the jungle. Nothing else on the road even came close.

She followed the sights and sounds all the way to Barnacle Bay. She hadn't been this far down on the Maroon County shoreline since a few summers ago when she and Serafina took a few weeks off together. Memories flooded back and ripped the strings of her heart apart. So much had changed. She couldn't think about any of it now, or she would turn her car around and go home to drown in her own pity pool.

Instead, she turned off her lights and eased onto the sand-covered, gravelly roadway. Alex had parked. She could see his taillights up ahead. Not many people ventured onto Barnacle Bay at that time of night, so she would have to be careful not to be seen or heard.

She parked about a half mile away from where his car had

pulled over. After locking up her truck, CJ sprinted into the dunes. She was careful to weave her way through the thick brush until she was less than one hundred feet from where they were parked. She could barely see anything. It was pitch black. But the moon reflecting on the water in combination with the ambient light from his car allowed her to see clearly the worst thing she had ever laid eyes on.

Alex sat in the driver's seat, which he reclined almost all the way back. Hayden was on top of him, straddling him. They were making out like teenagers. It looked as real as anything she had ever seen before. Her anger raged through her like a disease. She couldn't sit there and watch this. She had to do something.

Against any judgment, she pulled her fire thrower off her belt holster and sprinted toward his car. Only a few feet away, hidden in the brush, she took a large rock and threw it at the car. It bounced off the door, making a horrible sound but not looking like it left a mark.

Hayden stirred, and then jumped off of Alex. They both got out of the car. He was on the driver's side, but Hayden was on the side closest to CJ. She had one shot to kill before her own life ended. If she failed, it would mean she had done the unthinkable. If she succeeded, she would have to face the consequences.

CJ didn't care. It would all end tomorrow anyway.

She lifted her demon killer, aimed and heard Hayden scream her name.

"CJ, you little bitch!"

Alex rushed over to Hayden's side of the car to see what she was talking about. CJ didn't waste a moment on second thoughts. Alex was about five feet away. It took only a split second to aim. Then she pulled the trigger.

But Alex was too close. Much too close.

The moment the fireball hit Hayden, she burst into

flames. Her gorgeous body turned into ashes instantly, landing in a pile on the ground. Alex screamed and turned toward CJ, but she could already see it was too late. A wind gust arrived at the perfect time. One of the flames from Hayden's explosion traveled far enough to attach itself to Alex. In the second before he exploded, he caught CJ's gaze. She could have sworn his expression was more than horror—it was terrible regret.

"Oh my God. No." CJ ran over to his car and fell to the ground. "What have I done? Dear Lord, what have I done?" She picked up his ash, watching it slip through her fingers. "Alex, Alex, please. Come back to me. I'm so sorry. I didn't mean to hurt you. Come back, Alex. Come back." Her sobs were unrecognizable to her. She hadn't experienced the emotions that took over in almost a year. A thrust of rage, love, sadness and regret was all wrapped in a fiery package.

A car coming down the road interrupted her bout of grief. She crawled back on hands and knees, still weeping, into the nearby dunes. She crouched so she could watch the scene. The luxury sedan screeched to a halt next to Alex's car. Damon and Sera jumped out.

"Xander? Hayden? Where are you guys? We have the entourage coming. We need you. Guys? Hello?"

Sera made her way to the passenger's side of the car first. The moment she looked down, she nearly collapsed. "Damon, come quickly."

Damon met Sera and saw what was left of his two friends. "Watch your back." He pulled out his elixir gun. Sera followed suit.

CJ was still crying. She couldn't help herself. She hadn't intended to kill him. Now an entourage was coming. She wouldn't make it out of there alive.

Damon spoke into what looked like his collar. "Xander and Hayden are dead. No mercy."

No mercy? What did that mean?

CJ watched as Damon and Sera ran to the middle of the beach. CJ had no idea what they were doing, but she had to follow. No one was there to help her, but maybe if she put out a plea to Sera, her old friend would find it in her heart to spare her.

Moments later, it was as if the President of the United States had arrived. Car after car pulled up onto the sandy dunes, and what looked like ten people assembled. She watched as they seemed to be dragging humans the entire way.

CJ's heart beat like crazy. Damon and Sera stood guard over a hole in the ground, where demons were tossing humans. Loud thumps followed screams until the next carload got in line. Her old friend and boyfriend didn't seem to mind. She was sure Alex's and Hayden's murders didn't help their opinion concerning humans. There was no way they would pardon CJ. Not after the way she had acted and not after what she had done to their friends.

CJ peeked through the weeds to try and see who had been kidnapped. It made no sense. Why were they doing this now? The realization hit her hard. They had learned about the demon hunter plot and were getting ahead of it. Alex hadn't ever been Alex. He was Xander all along.

It didn't make her feel any better for killing him, but it did make sense.

She formed a tiny hole with her fisted hand and peered through it, the fastest way to make a magnifying glass. She couldn't see much. It was insanely dark. All she heard at first were the humans screaming in fear and pain. Until a familiar voice made her stomach turn.

"CJ? CJ, if you're here and you can hear me, please help us!"

She would know the voice anywhere. It was Mandy. CJ

heard a crack as someone kicked her friend in the ribs. "Ceeeeee Jaaaay," her friend wailed her name. "Help me!"

The words brought her back to the prison Alison had built almost one year ago. The place she had been shackled to the ground. The place where she had almost died. When she had seen the true meaning of evil and what lengths someone would go to demonstrate their evil. Serafina had saved her, but she wouldn't have had to save her at all, and Alison would still be their friend, and nothing would have changed if Serafina had chosen humanity over evil.

CJ had to do something now. For all the wrong she had done, this was something good and right, and she needed to risk it all this one and only time. Her only defense was to go on the offensive. So she did.

CJ closed her eyes as she sprinted out of the dunes screaming, her firearm elevated. She fired off shot after shot of fireballs as she headed straight toward a crowd of demons.

CHAPTER 26

Wind gusts carried sand crystals as they whipped around the beach, whirling furiously through the night air. With her head pointed toward the stars, Sera stood guard in a stoic stance over the main entry point to the bunkers below ground. The majority of the heavy lifting had been done, thanks to Lorenzo's unyielding mission and leadership. Their only job now was to manage their Special Demon Forces teams as the van loads of demon hunters were delivered to the underground prison.

The initiative had begun and would continue well into the next day. Sera waved another leader off with his hunters. "Bastards."

"Try not to think about it." Damon ushered the screaming humans into the ground. "Wrong place. Wrong time."

"Let's go. We don't have all night," Sera yelled to her group.

A hunter kicked Sera on her way down and screamed, "Go to hell!"

Sera kicked her back, harder. The woman flew down the

stairs, smashing onto the concrete floor. "This is your hell now. You murderous bitch!"

The hunters' screams died down the further away they moved from Sera.

"They'll pay. I promise you." Damon threw his fist in the air.

"How will they pay when we don't know who they are?" Sera was enraged. She wanted to break every demon hunter's neck in sight. Who did they think they were? The judge and the jury? No, they were animals, wild and out of control, exactly like her. She couldn't keep herself in check all hopped up on the Blaze elixir. All she wanted was to murder, murder and murder some more.

"I know you're pissed off. I'm furious too. But we have a bigger mission tonight. Hold tight. We can let loose tomorrow when no one's in harm's way." Damon slowed the line down and gave orders like a general. "One by one. Calmly and safely down the ladder. We're not here to kill anyone. We want order and control. Slow and steady now." Damon made a motion with his hands to demonstrate to the demons how to lower the hunters into the bunkers without excessive force. Still, the humans kicked and fought the entire time. It wasn't as though the demons had to fight back. They were stronger than they had ever been.

"Screw that. They'll think we are weak if we stand around." Sera understood how power could go to a demon's head. Power and an insatiable hunger to inflict harm, two of the most uncontrollable urges even she had trouble subduing. It was a taste of the demon experience. She wanted more.

"Who cares what the hunters think? Your team will believe you're weak if you show your emotion." Damon continued directing the demon soldiers as he spoke.

Sera knew he was right. "I'm on the verge of exploding."

"You're not alone. You just have less experience than the

rest of us holding your urges in. Right now, your job is to keep these soldiers under control. They're looking to you for leadership. You're responsible for mentally motivating them. I'm here for the brute force. Let me handle it, okay?"

"Fine." Sera wasn't happy about how any of it was going. She was on the edge of madness trying to hold it all in and failing fast.

"Phase two can't be implemented until we're certain every single hunter has been captured and is confirmed to be under full demon control. We've only just begun. Hang tight. This is it, Sera. You have to exercise complete self-discipline of the highest order."

"Got it." Sera carried a know-it-all attitude. She was well aware of it, in fact. Damon reminded her for good reason. She was out of control and they both knew it. All civilians would be drugged by the time they were kidnapped. However, they also posed a threat since demons couldn't be sure how each of them would react. They were sure some might be powerful enough to fight back despite the Blaze, while others would acquiesce like sleeping babies.

The hunters, however, hadn't been drugged. They were taken in the dead of night against their will. And no mind control was allowed. It was meant to be a brutal fight. Purposeful. People were meant to die, just not any demons. Especially not their friends, Xander and Hayden.

"What are you doing?" Damon yelled.

"Stop." Sera turned in the direction of a group of demons running toward the shore. It looked like they had about five hunters in tow.

"Get back here." Damon ran after them.

"Damon, stop."

Damon turned around. "They're not following the rules. We have to stop them."

"No, we don't. I need you here. Let them do whatever it is they're going to do and come back to help me."

Damon looked furious. She had rank over him, regardless of what he wanted to do. Besides, he trusted and respected her and wasn't going to betray the relationship they had established. He made his way back to her. They looked on as the demons proceeded to drown the hunters in the ocean.

"You can't be serious."

"I'm as serious as Santa."

"Santa is a myth."

"So you think."

"Fine. What are you trying to prove? By letting them veer off course and act in any way they want, you're showing a lack of leadership."

"Leadership isn't about making all of the decisions. It's about letting your people, who you've trained, decide for themselves what's best. For whatever reason, they've decided murdering those hunters was a better solution than keeping them captive. Who am I to argue?"

Damon shook his head. "That's not what this is about, is it?"

Damon knew her too well. She couldn't hide anything from him. "You told me not to show my emotions. So I'm not."

"You're not acting emotional, but you sure as hell are showing your emotions."

Sera shrugged and turned back to the task at hand. "Down the hole. Let's move it. Drop 'em and get back on the road for more."

"One at a time." Damon stomped his foot in demand.

Sera the motivator. Damon the controller. It was the liberating role reversal they both needed.

An outcry Sera recognized all too well pulled her attention front and center. A small figure all dressed in black stormed out from the dunes and was headed right toward them. Fireballs shot into the air, one after another. Demons ducked for cover frantically. They darted and dashed like bats in the night, feverishly attempting to avoid the same fate Xander and Hayden had suffered. The Blaze serum would help, but only for so long. They were trained not to take any chances.

Damon snatched Sera and they dove straight down into the bunker, hiding below the surface of the earth, away from the barrage of fire. When they landed at the bottom, they weren't alone. One after one, demons plunged to the ground behind them.

Sera pushed away from him and began climbing back up.

"What are you doing?" Damon grasped at her desperately.

"I need to be up there. I'm their leader."

"You'll get killed."

"So be it." Sera pulled her body up the ladder.

Damon grabbed her leg. "Sera, please."

She turned around, looking down at him. "I don't need you to save me." Sera tore away from Damon and heaved her body up and onto the beach. He didn't follow her. She had taught him to respect her wishes when she decided she must act alone.

The silence echoed in the open space. It was as if the mayhem had only lasted an instant. Severe and irreversible damage was done all the same. Tonight had gone terribly wrong. Where else had the agenda not gone according to plan? She shook off the thoughts and stepped far away from the entrance to the bunker and arm's reach.

Sera made her way around the barren beach to assess the gravity of the casualties. Giant piles of ash were strewn all over. It was the epitome of death and destruction. The remains of demons were not only ones that littered the sand; lifeless human bodies were scattered everywhere. Blood-soaked sand made a watercolor canvas of Barnacle Bay, its pinks and reds mixed with the tan undertones resembling an east coast horizon at dusk in the summertime. It was as beautiful as it was morbid.

The demons hadn't used the Blaze-filled weaponry. Instead, the ammunition was comprised of real, bonafide bullets. Her demon soldiers had shot to kill. Sera couldn't blame them. Many of her kind had lost their lives. Lorenzo's plan to fight fire with water was one the demons were destined to lose.

It wasn't like they had a choice in the matter. Demons needed to defend themselves. Whoever started the senseless slaughter was ruthless, and Sera was going to make them pay.

Several of the vans were gone. She hoped the remainder of her crew had taken them out to get more hunters. The mess had to be cleaned up in the meantime before the next round arrived. She would need help. Not much had been beneath her as a human, but moving dead bodies in her supernatural life wasn't going to happen.

A genius idea entered her brain. It was the first proactive thought she'd had in long time. It began to take shape in front of her eyes. In a macabre scene, each of the dead hunters' bodies lifted straight up off of the beach. They floated in unison toward the raging ocean. Sera could hardly believe her vision had come to life so perfectly.

Pleased, she took a step back. She crossed her arms as she waited for each corpse to plummet into the middle of the ocean, disappearing in the rough gray waves forever.

Satisfied with the ease of her mental cleanup, Sera turned and headed for the bunker to give her teams an update so they could all continue on with her mission. One setback did not make a failure.

That's when she heard it. The tinny voice from her childhood. The one that had died long ago when Jenna made the decision to become her enemy, CJ.

"How do you live with yourself?" CJ wavered on her feet, shaken.

Sera turned slowly to face her nemesis, unsure of what she would find. She saw a scared little girl hiding behind a giant assault weapon. CJ's hair was bloodied and stuck to her head, mixed with sweat and tears. The mascara streamed down her face, away from practically swollen-shut eyes. The leader of the demon hunter's black ensemble was ripped and burnt, exposing bloodied scars.

Sera had to admit her old friend had put up a suitable fight. Hands on hips, she responded in a frigid tone.

"I'd like to ask you the same question."

CJ's laugh was gurgled. "You're a killer."

Sera rolled her eyes. "Again, same for you." Her hand moved slowly to her side.

CJ shook as she moved toward Sera in a calculated motion. The oversized gun was aimed right at Sera's heart.

"I tried to warn you. I tried. I really did. But you wouldn't listen to me. You didn't want to hear it. You," CJ laughed bitterly, "you wanted to reconcile with me." CJ slowly progressed forward in agitated jerks. "Now look at what you've done."

"I haven't done anything. Everything went smoothly until you arrived and screwed it all up."

CJ broke down crying. "Me? I came here to—"

"What *are* you doing here?" Sera was confused.

"I came here..." Her gun was off balance, like someone trying to take a video with an unsteady hand. "He was with her..." CJ hyperventilated between her words, unable to get a full sentence out. "I didn't mean to...but I..."

Sera put two and two together.

"You came here for Xander."

"No." CJ shook her head and then nodded. "Yes."

Sera's fury took on a life of its own. She was seconds away from using her powers on CJ, but something in her mind blocked her ability to do so. Sera wanted the whole story. She wanted the truth, an admission straight to her face. Sera took a step forward.

"What happened to Xander and Hayden?"

"I saw them, in the car and..." CJ wiped her nose with the back of her arm and dropped her gun slightly. She lifted it back up and readjusted it until it was aimed directly at Sera.

CJ controlled her tone. "I wanted her out of the way. I thought if I could get rid of her, Alex and I could be together forever. That's what he wanted, you know? To be with me. Not her. He chose me. Not that demon whore."

Sera cocked her head. "Who's Alex?"

"Xander. He was Alex to me. We were in love. Meant to be. He was too close to Hayden. Damn it, why did he get so close? It was that demon bitch's fault. She's the one who killed him. It wasn't his time to die. We were supposed to be together. Forever."

CJ's gun began to fall with her tears, but then she lifted herself up, in fight mode again. Sera finally understood. CJ had killed Hayden and Xander in a fit of jealous rage, and then she had gotten caught in the crossfire. No matter, CJ had no right to try to take Sera's life. She wouldn't let the insane person Jenna had become destroy everything Sera had worked so hard for as an Ensoul.

"You're the one who killed Xander and Hayden? You murdered them both, didn't you? You started this. The blood-shed here is yours. Remember that."

CJ burst into tears. Irrational sadness emerging from behind her twisted expression.

"I didn't mean to do it. I only intended to kill her. Alex was too close. He shouldn't have gotten so close."

For a brief moment, Sera had the urge to run over and hug her old friend, to comfort terrible pain out of her. She wished she could take away Jenna's tears like she always had. She reminded herself how Jenna died, just like CJ had said, not so long ago. Directly in front of Sera now was CJ, a demon-killing murderer who used her selfish romantic desires as a justification to take people's lives. Sera had no place for CJ in her life.

Sera got closer. "You did it all. This is all your doing. Not mine or anyone else's. Now you're the one pointing a gun at me. I'm the person who saved your miserable life. What kind of human being are you? No, please don't answer me...I'll tell you. You're worse than an evil demon. You're the worst kind of evil. You are a self-serving, judgmental, righteous person who thinks she knows better than anyone else. Look at what you have done. You've killed the man you loved, and you're getting ready to kill the only person who truly cared about you. How does that make sense?"

"You're wrong. You started this war the day you turned into a supernatural evil being. You made me into this person. You did this to me."

CJ backed up a step as if she didn't want to get too close, but she kept her gun steady to show she had the upper hand. Sera gestured around the bloodied beach.

"On the contrary. Look around, CJ. The hatred for our species is proven by the dead bodies on the ground. Your selfish ways led to all of these deaths. You, and only you, have their innocent blood on your hands."

In the next breath, CJ's demeanor changed entirely. She got control of herself. It was as if she remembered something that changed everything. CJ's expression tensed. Her face grew bright red with fury.

"You're the one who took Mandy. I saw her get tossed into that hole as she screamed for me to save her. And those dead bodies you so carelessly disposed of...they were people. They had beating hearts. They were my friends. They were human beings who believed in me when no one else did. They're the reason I became the strong leader I am today. You threw them out like the Monday morning trash."

"You're wrong, old friend. This, right here, is the epitome of war. This is what war looks like. There's death and then there's more death. There's no room for friendship. No room for sympathy." She walked a few steps closer. "I'm doing what needs to be done. I suggest you do the same."

A smile crossed CJ's face. She resembled Jenna for the briefest of moments. Then the evil, the same evil that had lived in Alison the day she almost took Sera's life, flashed in shadows behind CJ's eyes. Her gaze fixated on something behind Sera. She glanced back to find Damon rising from the bunker in what seemed like slow motion. By the time Sera looked back in CJ's direction, the leader of the demon hunters had her weapon pointed at Sera's lover's head. There was no time for Sera to react.

CJ pulled the trigger.

With Sera's left foot, she thrust Damon back into the ground. Several fireballs whooshed past her head, searing off some of her hair. Without thinking, her right hand, already on her waist holster, instinctively whisked out the gun she hoped to never use and lifted it straight up into the air.

Sera did the unthinkable. She opened fire all over the demon hunter.

CHAPTER 27

OCTOBER 27, 1998

R afaela, Vera and Serafina stormed the food court. They were utterly famished after the long movie ended. It was their monthly girls' date, and this time it was Serafina's pick. She chose the latest vampire movie, which was way too long in Rafaela's opinion.

About halfway through the meal, someone called out Vera's name in a singsong voice. "Oh, Vera, darling! Is that you?"

Vera covered her face. "Not now."

"Who is that?"

Vera had no time to answer. The woman appeared at their table faster than anyone click-clacking in four-inch heels ever had.

Rafaela knew what the gorgeous pearlescent color of her irises meant. The truth was, it wasn't only her eyes that were stunning. Simply everything about her was breathtaking. Her lush black hair. Her bronzed skin. Those full lips. Rafaela was instantly jealous.

"Vera, please don't tell me you're eating at the mall food

court." She flung her hair back. "What are you, slumming now?"

"Alison, we'll talk later."

"We will talk now, as a matter of fact."

The woman who called herself Alison leaned on their table with both hands as if bearing down on them. Vera was visibly uncomfortable, her rigid demeanor telling the story to Rafaela. All the while Alison was having a conversation with Vera, her eyes never left Rafaela. She often looked away, making small talk with Serafina, who seemed to pay the woman no mind. Yet Alison's gaze was fixed on Rafaela like she was a bug to exterminate.

Alison's smile was devious. Her glare insidious. Rafaela wanted nothing more than to crawl under the table and hide or run. But she had her daughter to consider. Rafaela refused to be weak.

Finally, after Alison name-dropped Lorenzo a dozen times too many, Vera ended the conversation and forcibly walked Alison away. The whole time, Alison's head was turned back, watching Rafaela's and Serafina's every move. A sense of malice swarmed around her. Something was off, and it didn't sit well with Rafaela.

When Serafina wasn't paying attention, Rafaela got right to the point with Vera.

"What's Alison got against me?"

"It's complicated."

"Why am I not surprised?"

"Because nothing is easy or straightforward in our lives, and in your situation, even more so."

"Should I be worried?"

Vera's face darkened. "You and Serafina are off limits to demon harm."

"Again, I ask, should I be worried?"

"There will always be demons who resent you for your

angel pendant and Serafina's blood. But no matter how they feel, they simply cannot hurt you."

It gave Rafaela some relief. However, the gnawing deep within her bones told her otherwise.

"Say what you will, but if Alison wanted to cause harm, she would cause harm. She doesn't seem to care about consequences."

"You should know that Alison has a thing for Lorenzo."

Rafaela's heart sank. It bothered her. She swallowed hard. "Who doesn't?"

"It's more than attraction. Alison wants to be Lorenzo's protégé. She has been chasing him since she took her first breath and she has no intention of stopping any time soon."

Rafaela showed Vera her wedding ring. "I'm married now. Why is Alison concerned with me? I'm not in the way."

Vera's head tilted toward the little girl.

Serafina.

"And," Vera said, "you're the only woman Lorenzo ever truly cared about. The fact that you're human makes it even worse in Alison's eyes. And having had a child with him? Worse yet."

"Perfect."

"So, you're right. Alison is evil; she's the worst there is. But you have nothing to fear because both you and that beautiful little girl of yours are untouchable."

Rafaela smiled convincingly, but she believed Vera was wrong. Alison intended to harm them, and she would be successful. In what way and how badly, Rafaela couldn't speculate. The only caveat was Alison needed to be creative in her malice, which Rafaela had no doubt was possible.

Alison would do her damage. It was only a matter of time.

CHAPTER 28

PRESENT DAY

Sera dropped the gun to the ground. Her body followed close behind it. The reality of what had happened hit her like a tsunami. Damon made his way onto the beach and fell beside her. It had all come to a head in a matter of hours. It overwhelmed her. She was exhausted in more ways than she could describe.

"Is she dead?" Sera winced.

Damon nodded. "Yeah." He rubbed the place where the fireball had burned her shoulder. "Are you all right? You got hit straight on."

Sera swallowed hard. "I'm good."

"Thank you. I know what you did wasn't easy."

"I didn't even think. I reacted. I wasn't going to let anything happen to you." She closed her eyes and replayed the scene in her mind. It couldn't have taken longer than a few seconds to take the life, albeit a ruined one, of someone she had loved for years. Times had changed. No one was who they used to be. Sera was okay with it for the very first time.

"I would have done the same for you."

"I know it."

"I have to ask, only because of who she is, but what should we do with the body?"

Sera sat up. "I'll take care of it.

"Are you sure?"

"I know what she would've wanted."

Sera slipped back into the bunkers. By now, the demon leaders had organized the hunters who hadn't been killed into prison cells. A few stayed behind while Sera sent the others up and out to get more hunters.

"Mandy? Where's Mandy?" Sera weaved her way through the prison to find CJ's good friend. "Hello, is Mandy here?"

A voice down a long corridor echoed. "Where's CJ? I want to see her. What have you done with her, you psychotic bitch?"

Sera swallowed hard. She rolled her shoulders back and headed down the dark hallway to where she thought Mandy's voice was coming from.

"Mandy, where are you?"

The bars in a cell on the left shook. "Over here. Where is she? Where's CJ?"

Sera pulled up to the cell. "Listen to me. There's been a fight."

"Is she okay?"

Sera shook her head.

"No!" Mandy collapsed in tears.

Sera's heart broke with Mandy's. She had made the right choice, but it was still hard to face. Mandy would never understand. Sera respected her long-time, deranged friend for leading a cause bigger than herself, even if it was one she vehemently opposed. She reached to unlock the barred prison door.

A guard grabbed her arm. "What are you doing?"

Sera ripped away from him. "Don't put your hands on me."

The guard took a few steps back. "I'm protecting you. These demon hunters are killers."

"Yes, I'm aware. So are we." Sera opened the door and led Mandy out. She was handcuffed but still a fighter. The guard was right. Mandy was a threat. "I'll take you to her."

"What happened?" Mandy's grief hid her fury.

Sera didn't answer. Instead, she guided Mandy out with a guard following close behind. "Come."

When they got to the surface, no explanation was needed. Sera and Mandy stepped around the destruction. It was a war zone. The smell of death permeated the air.

Two enemies walked together, side by side through the sea of dead bodies, for the sake of a dear friend.

When they reached CJ, Mandy and Sera lowered themselves to the sand instinctively. Sera behind CJ's head, and Mandy at her feet. The demon guard approached slowly, but Sera put her hand up. She needed a minute.

Dark, uneven bloodstains covered her old friend, ones Sera herself had caused. Be it right or wrong, she had done it to save a life, even one belonging to a demon. She didn't regret it, not even as Sera brushed the hair away from the demon hunter's closed eyes. She had done what was necessary to survive.

Sera expected CJ's face to be frozen in pain, but it wasn't. She looked at peace. And a lot like Jenna Cassidy. In many ways, she *was* at peace now—with her higher power. No matter CJ's sins, Jenna had risen above in the afterlife. It had never been her fault. In truth, demons had caused all of her pain, which prompted her to do the things she did. Sera put her hands on the crown of her friend's head, recalling an old prayer from the confessions of her youth.

Mandy bowed her head in prayer. It was as if she was the one who could read minds and knew exactly what Sera said in her thoughts. The spirit of the body before them was surely in a better place than the two of them were at that moment. For those left behind, there was no place to escape the hate. It was everywhere.

As the hunter and the hunted stood, roles now reversed, no words were exchanged. Instead, they did what needed to be done. In unison, they lifted CJ up in silence. They carried her in the silent memorial from the sand to the shore. When they reached the ocean, both walked into the water, small waves crashing against their legs. They laid down the girl with the given name Jenna Cassidy. Jenna floated, rocking on top of the sea until she disappeared in her grave far into the ocean she loved so much.

Once they could no longer see her, Mandy and Sera made their way back to the underground, the demon guard leading the way. Mandy, shoulders low, said, "She never stopped loving you. I didn't understand it, and CJ would never admit it, but I saw it in her eyes every time she spoke your name."

Sera glanced over, hiding the admiration in her expression. "CJ wasn't Jenna. She was a killer. Like me."

Sera acknowledged how much alike the two old friends had become. Both had changed, yet instead of joining forces, they had become mortal enemies. The two little girls from long ago would never have guessed how their lives would turn out, which had been better off for them both.

"CJ was traumatized, so no, she wasn't Jenna. But she had the same heart. She didn't want to become this...a murderer, this proponent of hate, but the choice didn't belong to her. Society and the evil it had become turned her into the hunter, and a damn good one at that. She said she hated you, and you were everything the hunters stood against, but it was all a ruse. I saw it in her eyes. She wanted nothing more than to go back in time, but that wasn't possible. All she had was the here and now, and it was full of war and hate and death. She had to pick a side. There was no way she couldn't fight for her people. She couldn't become the very thing, the very evil that had turned her into a desperate and unstable person." Mandy stopped a few feet from the bunker. "She wasn't going to become like you." Mandy's cold and unforgiving eyes said it all.

Sera hadn't said anything to Mandy about how CJ had died, but Mandy understood. Even if Sera hadn't heard it in her thoughts, she read it in the expression on Mandy's face.

"Let's go."

Sera gestured for the guard to take Mandy into the ground. They may have shared a moment, but nothing was going to change the reality of their world, a world that had turned best friends against each other and made every human being into a potential killer.

Right before Mandy's head dipped below the earth, she called out. "I have something for you."

Sera leaned down and shouted at the guard, "Hold it." She looked at Mandy. "What is it?"

Mandy's eyes darted down. "It's in my bra."

Sera raised her eyebrows. "Excuse me?"

"The second half of your note. It's from Jenna."

It was the first time Mandy had called her something other than the leader of the demon hunters. Sera knew exactly what Mandy was talking about. A van pulled up behind them, and a swarm of demons with hunters in tow fell out, rushing the bunker. Round two had begun. It was going to be a long night.

Sera reached into Mandy's shirt without hesitation and found the note, whipping it out. "Thank you."

Mandy looked away and followed the guard back to her prison cell. This time, she didn't fight.

Damon must have heard the commotion because the moment Sera had cleared the bunker opening. He was right next to her.

"You alright?"

"I'm good," Sera said.

"What's that?" Damon pointed at the paper crumpled in Sera's hand.

"A note. From Jenna."

"Jenna?" Damon looked confused.

Sera nodded. "Can you handle this mania on your own, get everyone settled down there?"

"No question. Go, read your note. Let me know if there's anything I can do."

Sera turned to leave. Damon spun her around, pulling her close. He whispered in her ear, "Don't let this break you." He kissed her hard and let her go.

Sera was off balance but took the sentiment with her as she strolled off toward the sea where Jenna's body had found its final resting place.

With chaos all around her, she unfolded the note and read it to herself.

Serafina,

I know that's not what you call yourself these days, but I figured if you were reading this, it didn't matter. I'd be dead, and hanging on to pretenses in the afterlife made no sense at all.

If I'm dead, it's likely because you or someone in your regime killed me. Ironic, isn't it? Best friends going for blood? I guess I shouldn't be surprised with how things panned out for us last year. You're this evil being, and I'm a murderer.

However, there's more to our story, old friend. Had I told you everything when I was alive, I know you wouldn't have believed a word of it. You've built an enviable life for yourself, one of power, wealth and immortality. It's part of the reason I became your enemy. There's no way we'd be able to go back to the way things were before.

You befriended Alison so easily, often times putting her before me, and then killed her while saving my life, which confused me. I didn't know if I could trust you. Would you kill me one day, too? Then when you became what you are now, it was clear. You made the decision to become what Alison was—a demon—and I would never accept it. You made my decision clear. Be the hunted, or be the hunter. I chose the latter. Our friendship died with our new identities.

As it turns out, it was never me you had to worry about. It's true. I was a demon hunter. I'm proud of what I became. But the truth is, I lived on the defensive.

Lorenzo is the one who built and sustained the bunkers. Not the demon hunters. He used humans to create them. His demons had nothing to do with it. But I knew. It was one of the reasons my hunters hated you so much. We assumed you and Damon were in on it.

Your biological demon father lied to you. He's a fraud.

Why would you believe me? Because believing me will save your life.

I didn't orchestrate your attack. Lorenzo was responsible. He drugged me and controlled my mind until I was temporarily addicted to violence, especially against you.

He was and is plotting, Serafina. Only this time, it's against you. You're his biggest threat as the only other Ensoul alive.

Make no mistake, Lorenzo's ruthless beyond measure. No matter what I've said to you, we both know you're nothing like him.

I wish things had been different. We had a good life once. We loved each other.

Whatever you decide to do with this information is up to you. So ask yourself, will you die for the ones you love or the ones who love you? What evil will you truly become? Or can you turn it all around? Can you break the cycle of evil?

I know what Serafina would do.

Jenna

The commotion behind her hadn't let up, but Sera stood silent and still, shaking slightly. Her body twitched and muscles flexed involuntarily. *What have I done?* She squeezed her eyes together until they hurt and swallowed the last of her loyalty. She understood everything now, it all made perfect sense. The note in the hospital and everything leading up to this moment.

She crumpled her best friend's letter and tossed it into the ocean to die along with Jenna. The proof wasn't needed. In truth, she had never needed any evidence, just the confirmation of what was already in her heart. The one and only thing she would ever need again would be to trust in herself. No piece of paper would make it happen.

She turned on her heels and ran to Damon. "Get coverage."

"What's going on?" Damon didn't only wear grave concern on his face but all over his body.

"We need to see Lorenzo. Now."

Rafaela knew she would die soon. Michael told her she was letting Alison win. The demon was out to get her. It wasn't paranoia. It was her reality.

Rafaela couldn't leave the house without running into Alison. She was always trailing three steps behind. At first, Rafaela assumed it was a coincidence, but she was wrong. Alison had been following her.

She was even in Rafaela's dreams.

Vera confirmed a demon's ability to enter a human's mind while they were sleeping. It was different than when the human was awake; Rafaela's angel pendant blocked Alison.

But when Rafaela was asleep, Alison had an entrance into Rafaela's mind, an entrance of intense worry and fear opened, and no pendant could protect her.

Popping up regularly in Rafaela's world, Alison had designed it so that there was no way to stop thinking about her or stop fearing her.

In Rafaela's dreams, Alison waited, looming over her in sleep as she did in life. Alison was the shadowy image blurred and just out of sight. She was nowhere, yet she was everywhere.

Because of this, Rafaela knew the end was near. Alison was coming for her, if not in life while awake, then to kill Rafaela in her dreams, and soon.

The dreams with Alison were nothing compared to the recurring nightmare that haunted Rafaela, the same one she had every night.

It started out on a beautifully sunny day. Rafaela was standing at the window with the breeze surfing into the house. She was content watching Serafina play in the backyard. Her daughter was a little girl, maybe five years old and as innocent and adorable as she was today. Her long hair was full of buoyancy as she flew high into the air on her swing set. She was laughing, and Rafaela could see it on her face and hear it on the wind. She was smiling, too, because her heart was fuller than it had ever been. Michael was right by her side, and he wrapped his loving arms around her, and they stared at their precious child having the time of her life.

As if all at once, the darkest of clouds rolled in. It was as if they were suddenly in a horror movie. The storm raged out of nowhere. Serafina was caught it in. They ran to her, but they never made it in time. No matter how many times Rafaela had the dream, they never got to Serafina in time. When the lightning struck, Serafina went flying off the swing set. She soared high up into the sky, disappearing, until moments later when her little body slammed into the ground. She would be lying face down in the grass. They ran to her, and when they finally turned her over, they knew she was gone.

But that was not even the most terrifying part for Rafaela. The worst part of all was that her lifeless eyes were open. They were the eyes of a demon.

In the next scene, it was years in the future. Oddly, everything looked the same to Rafaela. She was no longer an active participant in the dream but merely an observer.

Serafina was older, a professional person, in her dress suit getting ready for work. Michael was in his recliner reading the paper. He had lost all of his hair. Rafaela couldn't tell if it was due to old age or an illness.

Either way, Serafina was beautiful. She could only see part of her face at first because she was looking down. Rafaela wanted to reach out and touch her, wrapping her arms around her daughter, but she couldn't. Rafaela was not in the dream because she was not alive any longer. There was a sadness looming over the two people she loved the most. It was her loss plaguing them. Their lives had never been the same since she passed, which she assumed was years prior. They were both well adjusted. There was no grief, only a weight upon them. Her absence had changed them, and she was powerless to do anything about it.

Right before Rafaela awoke, she reached out to put her hand on Serafina's shoulder. And while she couldn't see Rafaela, Serafina could feel her touch this time. When Rafaela spun Serafina around, it was Rafaela who was surprised. Serafina was beautiful, but she was a demon. Rafaela couldn't help but scream. Serafina heard her, but all she could do was cry.

The nightmare was Rafaela's future, one that haunted her, one that broke her heart every single night. And one she was powerless to change.

CHAPTER 30

PRESENT DAY

Te he front door to Lorenzo's oversized three-story mansion on the Nautical River exploded. Sera's rage was what shredded the Italian handcrafted double-wooden custom masterpiece into the tiniest splinters imaginable. She rushed through the foyer, a tornado swirling around her.

"You manipulative bastard. Where are you?"

On the short ride from the beach, as demon hunters were getting taken in the night and humans were drugged, Sera filled Damon in on all she had learned from Jenna. She saw the understanding in his eyes and was thankful he hadn't said *I told you so.* Some things were better left for Sera to figure out all on her own, and then address the consequences head on. With every step Sera took, it was as if all of her powers were activated at once. There were no other humans or demons in the house—she couldn't hear their thoughts.

Damon scoured each room for Lorenzo. He was nowhere to be found. "We're here for the truth."

His demands were less disrespectful than Sera's, but he had years under Lorenzo's rule and understood how the man worked. Lorenzo's betrayal had dropped the floor out from under Sera. Suddenly, Sera knew exactly where Lorenzo was. Of course, he would be basking in the glory of his world-dominating success in the only place he held dear.

Sera ran to Damon and pulled him toward the hallway. "Down here."

The steel basement door crumpled off of its hinges, forming itself into a ball that rolled down the stairs. Sera and Damon took off after it through the dark and steep, narrow staircase into the earth. It was an abyss for humans that doubled as Lorenzo's cave. Sera had never been there, but Damon had told her of the many rituals performed in earlier days when Lorenzo was focused on uniting his demon regime. With a strong and dedicated army, rites were conducted on a much less frequent basis.

As they reached the first level, Sera couldn't see anything anymore. The walls were caving in on them, getting smaller and smaller. Thank goodness the claustrophobia hadn't carried over from her human life.

She hesitated, slowing, and Damon reassured her. "Keep going. There's only one way in and one way out of here. It's tight, but you can't get lost. Feel along the walls, trace them with your hands. You might not be able to run, but you can use touch to weave your way through the tunnels."

"I have to give it to him. The man is a genius. Unless a hunter had a death wish, no one would come down here even if they knew there was something to find."

Sera placed her palms flat on the walls and walked as quickly as she could. The halls twisted and turned into what seemed like knots, going ever deeper into the ground. They must have walked for miles, but Sera couldn't truly tell.

"We're almost there." Damon put his hand on her shoulder.

Fury and confusion filled Sera. "What are we going to do when we get there? I don't have a plan."

"You'll know what to do. You always know the right thing to do."

Sera stopped dead in her tracks. She spun around and wrapped herself around the man she loved. She kissed him with a passion that would have killed anyone else. He returned her enthusiasm.

"Wow. What was that for?"

"Because I love you." Sera caressed his arm. "And because I don't want an ounce of compassion in my soul when I see the devil himself."

"It sounds like you have your plan."

"No mercy."

Sera handed Damon a giant vial of Blaze, matching the one she saved for herself. They drank them rapidly. They would need all the strength they could get before facing the most powerful supernatural being in the world. Then they continued on their journey. A few minutes later the maze straightened out.

"We're here," Damon said.

Sera knew exactly what she needed to do. She sprinted as rapidly as her legs would let her. They went faster than she ever imagined. Damon kept up right behind her. A tunnel of gusty wind seemed to lift them up off the ground until they were floating, practically flying. They sped toward what looked like a brick wall. Just like her human dream before she chose evil.

"Keep going."

"I'm not stopping for anything."

Once they reached the end, the wall would disappear right before their eyes. She had been there before, even if only in her dreams. Sure enough, the moment they got within feet of the end of the tunnel, the layers of the stonewall began to disappear until the opening was visible. They shot up through the air as if flying until they landed on the other side.

"Welcome." Lorenzo leaned forward in his giant throne, brandy snifter in hand. "You made it. What took you so long?"

The symbol of all demons, wings on fire, raged with flames burning all around the room. It was a deadly obstacle course for demons. Lorenzo's purposeful lighting forced any visitor to pass through the flames to get to the obligatory stage. It was a death wish.

"A little thing called murder. It seems to happen a lot where you're concerned."

Sera took careful steps around the flames, in case she was wrong about her theory. She glanced back and saw Damon doing the same. The elixir would help curb any small flames from killing him, but she wasn't sure about more than that, or if Lorenzo had rigged the fire. For good measure, Sera imagined the flames extinguished. Before the thought left her mind, it was as if a breeze took them all out. Except one. A giant symbol of wings on fire was lit above Lorenzo on the wall behind his throne. As Sera suspected, it wasn't the same fire as the others, or it would have also gone out. For fun, she concentrated on it, but nothing happened.

It was the only light left illuminating the dark space.

"You, my dear, are a force to be reckoned with. I've always said that." Lorenzo sat up with his glass goblet filled with clear liquid, obviously the elixir.

"You're drinking Blaze like wine? You're crazier than I thought." Sera stepped up to greet Lorenzo as if they were going to spar. She sensed a fight of some kind was coming.

Lorenzo stood to face her. He towered over her. It would have seemed confrontational, yet his demeanor was relaxed. "Crazy is as crazy does." His laugh was dark and sinister, one she recalled from her murderous demon friend, Alison, so long ago.

"I'm the crazy one. I believed your lies. You tricked me." The power of her emotions pushed Lorenzo back a step.

He caught himself from stumbling. He was drunk on his protective potion. "I am your truth, Sera. You haven't realized it yet."

Lorenzo glanced Damon's way, and he fell to the ground, then sprang back up to his feet. By the time Damon was at Sera's side, she had slammed Lorenzo against the wall in response. His goblet of elixir shattered, spilling all over the concrete. Lorenzo laughed. He seemed amused with her powers, proud even. He brushed himself off and stood.

"I see. You want to show me what you've got. Well, my dear, that isn't necessary. Because I already know. In fact..." He took a few steps closer. "You should be very proud of yourself."

Sera blinked, confused with where he was going in the conversation. "Proud? What are you talking about?"

Lorenzo carefully studied both of them before speaking. Sera was on display and her nerves had gotten to her. She wasn't going to like what he was about to say.

"Of your success. You did it." He smiled wider than she had ever seen, then laughed uncontrollably. "I was hoping, but I couldn't be sure. I mean, I knew you had it in you. Of course you did, you're my daughter. Still, the human influence, I wasn't certain. But, my lucky stars, you did it!"

Sera, now furious, screamed, "Did what?"

Damon put his hand on her back for a brief moment, letting her know he was there and on her side. Lorenzo was about to drop an atom bomb on her.

"You, Sera the Ensoul, passed the very last test."

Sera took a step back inadvertently. She wracked her

brain. "Test? What test?" Was it the war? The bunkers? Her team? She had no idea.

"Jenna. She was your last test."

Sera responded quickly. "Confronting CJ on the beach yesterday was the least of my accomplishments. What I want to know is—"

Lorenzo cut her off. "I didn't say CJ. I said Jenna."

That was when it clicked. Sera had interchanged CJ and Jenna so easily it didn't dawn on her. To be able to confront CJ was the easy part for Sera, but finding out she was Jenna and not killing her on the spot was much harder. According to Lorenzo, becoming her enemy was a step in the right direction for Sera. However, killing the person she loved most, Jenna not CJ, was the ultimate goal. It was the ultimate final exam.

Sera closed her eyes as she spoke, gaining perspective and control. "Jenna was right. Everything she said in the letter was true."

When Sera's eyes shot open, Lorenzo wasn't smiling anymore.

"Letter?" Lorenzo's tight brow exemplified concern.

"Yes. Your little anti-protégé told me everything in a letter she'd written before I blew her up all over Barnacle Bay."

Sera approached Lorenzo, controlling her mind and trying not to hurt him with her insane rage as she got her words out. She would confront him on his betrayal and destroy him. Damon kept pace next to her. Lorenzo, caught off guard, backed up until he fell into his throne.

"She's a liar. You know demon hunters are after us, all of us. They want to extinguish us from existence. You can't ever be safe in a world with humans. I've told you that from the beginning."

"No, you've told me what you wanted me to believe. You

never told me the truth."

Beware of the truth.

Embrace the truth.

Rafaela's words came rushing back to Sera. They were the same words carrying her through her decision to choose evil in order to fight it. Instead, she had embraced it in the wrong way. She had embraced her evil instead of embracing who she truly was inside. By embracing her inner demon, she was supposed to love the parts of herself she hated and wanted to deny. She was meant to merge them with the qualities she loved, to find some meaning in her existence and to live paving her own way, not the path Lorenzo had chosen for her.

It all came together now. Sera understood everything. And exactly what she needed to do.

Lorenzo waved his hands. "Listen to me. You're not thinking straight. Your human heart hasn't died yet, it's taking over. Don't listen to it. You'll kill us all."

There was fear in Lorenzo's eyes. Sera was in control.

"You're the liar. Humans never had a plan to imprison and torture us. You caused all of it. You built the bunkers, you created the elixir, and you developed an army of superior demons to take over the planet. Humans never had a chance. Their only mistake was thinking they could possibly protect themselves against you." Sera leaned over him. "And my only mistake was believing in you."

Sera backed up a step, but before she could think or act, there was a sinister glint in Lorenzo's eye. He scanned the room and one by one the wings on fire came to life with flames. Sera and Damon were momentarily distracted and it was enough for Lorenzo to attack. He lifted Damon up off of the ground using only his mind, then threw him into the center firepit and watched him burn.

Sera leaped to his rescue, leaving Lorenzo behind. Damon was alive, but the potency and volume of elixir he had drunk were the only things keeping him that way. She had no idea how long it would last and when he would burst into flames. Damon screamed in pain as his flesh burned.

"Let him go!" Sera tried to counteract Lorenzo's power, but her emotions were getting in the way. She couldn't concentrate.

"I'm fine. Get him. Do this, Sera. Please. For everyone you couldn't save."

Damon's skin melted. His bone was exposed. Her heart broke in spades. He would die any moment if she didn't do something. Lorenzo didn't play fair. He never had. He never would. This was the last straw. It was time to stop asking permission and to do what needed to be done.

Sera spun around. "You've gone too far."

Lorenzo smiled wide. "He was always in the way, Sera. This world was meant for you and me to rule. Damon was fat to be cut away. It's you who had the power all along. Don't waste it on a weak demon who makes an embarrassment out of all of us. He may as well be human."

She calmed herself and approached Lorenzo. "No, Lorenzo. It's you who has always been in the way."

Sera left Lorenzo standing exactly where he was, unable to see what she was doing. The metal structure of wings on fire hanging on the wall behind him, the one she couldn't extinguish, came crashing on top of Lorenzo.

He fell to the ground face first and then struggled to stand. "What's the matter? You're not a fan of fire?"

He laughed as his skin burned, never showing his pain, yet the intense fear in his eyes remained. "Fire won't kill me, Sera. Nor will a demon."

Sera suspected as much, but it was fun to see him writhe in pain. Damon's screams got weaker. He was fading fast. She glanced back, and his whole body was beginning to char. He couldn't have much time left. She had to do something.

If the fire wouldn't kill Lorenzo but he was clearly still afraid, Sera obviously posed a threat. Demons were the only ones who could truly kill other demons. But what about Ensouls? Sera was the only other Ensoul alive. Lorenzo had never shown fear with any other demon before, not even in an attack. She had seen him in action, even if only in video. They could have been staged, yet she had heard the stories of his bravery. Maybe it wasn't bravery at all? Maybe she was truly the only being who could take his life. She understood all at once.

"No. But I can. I'm the only one who can."

Lorenzo's eyes widened. Sera reached down and broke off a piece of the metal from the wings on fire burning. She kicked him over until she could see his face.

"I died to become like you. I thought my life would mean something simply because I was a supernatural being. But I was wrong. My destiny wasn't to become like you. It was to become like me. Serafina Murano, the human hybrid. More than an Ensoul, Lorenzo. That's something you'll never understand. A human spirit can never die. Humans are as immortal as demons, and they don't have to become an evil being to prove it. I guess I learned the hard way. And now it's time to make it right."

Sera lifted the metal bar above her head.

Lorenzo cried for the first time. "No, Sera. My beautiful daughter. Please don't do this. You don't understand. I love you."

Sera paused for the briefest of moments. "You don't know the first thing about love. This one's for my mother."

She slammed the bar with brute force straight into his heart. Blood spurted everywhere. Lorenzo twisted in pain. He could feel it. It was killing him as if one human were killing another.

To finish it off, Sera took the sharp end of a metal spike and placed it on the edge of his neck.

"And this one's for my father."

She pushed in a deep line with the point, slitting his throat. He gurgled, and blood came pouring out of his mouth. A moment later, he stopped moving.

Sera had killed the leader of all demons.

Lorenzo was dead.

All of the fires went out, except for the one under Lorenzo. Sera rushed to Damon's side. There wasn't much of him left, but she had to try to save him. She searched around and found exactly what she was looking for in the corner behind Lorenzo's throne: a carafe of elixir.

Sera poured the Blaze down Damon's throat. "C'mon. Please. Live, Damon. Drink this and live."

She waited, but nothing happened. Sera began to cry. It wasn't something she was comfortable doing. She hadn't cried since she was human. She hadn't known she could cry at all. She had no choice. The emotions she had all around—from murdering Jenna to the betrayal of her demon-leading father and now the potential death of the only love in her life—couldn't be held back.

Sera moved his burnt body to the concrete floor. She poured the elixir all over him and down his throat again.

"Please. Damon. Heal, damn it."

She waited. Still nothing.

Sera lifted him up, leaning him onto her, and poured the last of the liquid between his lips. She hoped it went down his throat with some pooling in his mouth. She held onto him crying, rocking him back and forth.

She whispered in his ear over and over again.

"I love you. Please don't leave me. Not now. I need you more than ever."

The grief from the loss of all of the people she had loved

—her mother, her father, Vera, Jenna—came rushing back. It was more than she could bear. For the first time as a supernatural being, she felt one hundred percent human again. After a few minutes, there was nothing more Sera could do for Damon. She would have to live with his loss as she had lived with the others.

She slowly slid away, laying him on the ground. Before she stood, she leaned over him one last time and gave him a kiss.

"I love you. You and me will always be."

She headed for the door. Before she stepped through the transparent wall, she heard a cough. Sera spun around. Had she not killed Lorenzo? She was on high alert.

Lorenzo hadn't moved an inch.

It was Damon. He coughed. She darted to his side. "I'm here. I'd never leave you."

Over the next few minutes, Damon came back from what seemed like the dead. His skin healed, and before long he was fully recovered and better than before.

"What happened?" He was groggy and confused.

Sera helped him stand. "The shit went down. I'll tell you all about it on our way back."

Arm in arm, they left their hell on earth.

CHAPTER 31

SEPTEMBER 13, 1994

After handing her newborn baby girl, Serafina, to the nurse, Rafaela grabbed a pen and pad and started to write.

Dear Serafina,

Happy birthday! Today is the day the most incredible miracle I've ever experienced has finally arrived. You.

First things first: I love you more than anything in this crazy world. I love all of the things you are and all of the things you'll become. I love the beautiful and intelligent woman you're destined to turn into.

But here's the reality: life is tough, Serafina. This is the truth you'll learn, and it's not a lesson for the faint of heart. There are times you'll soar through life without a care in the world, but more often than not, you'll struggle to make sense of it all. You'll question your existence. You'll want to know what it means to be good or to be evil.

Know this: no matter where your life takes you, you're loved more than anything in this world. More so, you've got the power to make your life whatever you want it to be, no matter how impossible it may seem at times.

When the odds are stacked against you, it's not the world you'll need to rely on...it's you. Push beyond the limits of your dreams until you're exactly the person you want to be, regardless of the risk or resistance from the world. You have everything inside of you needed to make your life amazing.

Be the inspiration. Be the change. Be all of it.

One last thought before I go, my sweet little baby girl, and one word for you to carry through your entire life, a word that means everything: Embrace. Embrace all things. Embrace the good and embrace the bad in your life, for they're both teaching you a lesson so you can grow. Most importantly, embrace YOU. You're a miracle, Serafina, and I'll love you for all of eternity.

All of my love, always and forever,

Mommy

CHAPTER 32

PRESENT DAY

"It's been one week since the world was set on fire, and not by the demon hunters, but by our world's new supernatural leader." The newscaster flashed to a picture of Sera releasing the imprisoned humans on Barnacle Bay the same night she had killed Lorenzo.

"They're making me into a hero." Sera looked away. "I'm no hero. I'm a murderer."

Damon wrapped his arm around Sera as they watched the latest broadcast on that fateful night. "You never give yourself enough credit. You saved all of them, Sera. Humans and demons. Lorenzo manipulated every single one of us, and you were the only person able to do what needed to be done. You should be damn proud."

Sera took a sip of her wine. "I never wanted this to be my life, you know. I wasn't looking for a starring role in the nightly news. I didn't ask for any of this."

"No, you didn't. But it was the destiny you could never have escaped. You may not have auditioned for the part, but you were chosen nonetheless. Now, you're in complete control of the person you'll become. Emulate the change you want the rest of the world to follow. All eyes are on you, my love."

Sera leaned into Damon. "What if I fail?"

Damon kissed the top of her head. "What if you flourish?"

Sera pulled Hope close, the dog already half on her lap, as they snuggled into Damon on the oversized leather couch. Sera still tried to make sense of everything she had done.

She raised the volume on the television. The evening news anchor, Donna Willis reported, "One week ago, no one would ever have known the devious plot Lorenzo of Enzo and Dell planned. Let's go to Annie Graham in the field. Annie, can you tell the viewers where you are?"

"Yes, Donna I certainly can." The camera flashed to the inside of the underground bunkers. Annie led an exclusive tour for the cameraman to capture the horror for all the world to see.

"I'm about fifty feet below the New Jersey shoreline right now standing inside one of the infamous prison cells originally designed to house and torture human beings indefinitely."

Annie turned around to the camera as she walked backward. "Hidden away below ground all over the globe, one supernatural leader manipulated the world into believing human beings were the enemy. These were the same human beings who had given demons equals rights all of those years ago. The injustice and lack of gratitude are impossible to understand." The field reporter shook her head. "To think we were moments away from demons taking over humanity is something none of us can truly fathom." Annie stood resigned as she faced the camera. "Back to you, Donna."

"On the heels of a potential mass destruction, a woman known as Sera, formerly Serafina Murano, has done the unthinkable. She murdered her own biological father to save the world and dedicated it all to the one person who betrayed her, Jenna Cassidy, a demon hunter leader who called herself CJ. While violence is never condoned, Sera did what had to be done for the good of mankind. And she's not even human. Jon Stapleman has more on the story."

"Donna, I'm standing here in the middle of New York City as they announce the planning stages to build a memorial for the lives lost merely one week ago. From those fighting for their human rights to the people who were drugged and kidnapped, the one person who brought it all to light was Jenna Cassidy."

"I miss her."

"She's been gone since Alison took her away from you. Jenna's been on a downward spiral for far too long."

"It's still tragic to me." Sera turned to Damon. "You're all I have left." Hope, as if she understood exactly what they were saying, whined. "And you, of course." Sera rubbed her husky's fluffy head.

The news went on about Jenna's life, the tragedy that struck one year ago and how she saved everyone with her letter. After her story, the next hour was dedicated to Sera and how she was the new supernatural, an Ensoul who was more like a human being than any demon had ever been.

Sera had been all over the news the day after the war on humans both began and ended. She had done the right thing and turned over all of Lorenzo's supplies of the Blaze serum. She revealed all of his secrets in her televised interview with Babs Quinn, the elite, powerful, lifetime achievement award-winning investigative reporter. Sera held nothing back and had been paid handsomely in trust for her honesty.

Declared the new ruler of the supernatural, Sera was given a key to New York City and every town along her beloved New Jersey shoreline. Sera became a celebrity, a hero and a badass who people all over the world now admired.

Of course, she was not at all comfortable with any of it. But she had made a commitment to serve humanity a long time ago when she chose to become a demon, a promise she never truly wanted to break. And if not for the manipulation of Lorenzo, she would have done.

Now, Sera vowed to make her life's mission to ensure the demons left behind on Earth were under her zero tolerance human servitude rule. To stay alive, they would need to manage their evil. If they were not successful, Sera would have no problem asserting herself and removing them from the world for all eternity.

Unlike life under Lorenzo's rule, Sera's leadership was entirely transparent. She earned the trust of human beings and had their full support as a result. This time, she had no intention of letting them down.

"It's surreal. I can't grasp the concept of it all yet." Sera shook her head, still in disbelief of how her life had come full circle.

Damon squeezed her tightly. "Not to me. I always knew what you were capable of doing. I've said from the very beginning you were much, much more than you could ever have imagined. We aren't here to imprison and take over humanity, even if they don't agree with us. We need to make them respect us, not by force but by our actions. You're the perfect example of it. You've proved to the world how even an otherwise evil demon, albeit a unique one, could be kind and do good things. You made the difference. All the difference in the world."

Sera raised her eyebrows. "I hope you're right. It's only just begun. I acted without thinking, and now I have so much responsibility. I hope I can live up to these expectations."

"You said it. You acted without thinking. You did what needed to be done. You're a true leader, and the very person this world needs to move forward at a time when things are fragile and in a state of upheaval. You know what's right, Sera. You've always known. And you've never hesitated in doing what needed to be done, no matter what the consequences were. You're as rare as your species and as unique."

Sera blushed. "Thank you, but it was Jenna who told me the truth. If it weren't for her letter, I would have gone through with all of it. She was the real hero.

"She was a hero in many ways, you're right. But you're the one who took action. You are the only one of us who consistently made the tough decisions from day one. And your decisions saved all of us."

Sera smiled. She should celebrate a little. "It's good to be saved."

"Finally, you're catching on."

"I'm so grateful to have you by my side."

"Where else would I be?"

"I don't know. You could be anywhere you wanted. But I'm over the moon you chose to live life alongside me."

"Always will," Damon said.

Sera kissed the wings on fire tattoo on Damon's forearm. "Well, my love, get ready. Because it's only the beginning."

THE END

ALSO BY KRISTINA RIENZI

ABOUT THE AUTHOR

Kristina Rienzi is a Jersey Shore-based new adult thriller author, certified professional coach, and the former president of Sisters in Crime-Central Jersey. An INFJ who dreams beyond big, Kristina encourages others (and herself) to embrace the unknown through her stories. When she's not writing or drinking wine, Kristina is spoiling her baby girl (and two fur-babies), dissecting true crime stories, singing (and  dancing) to Yacht Rock Radio, or rooting for the WVU Mountaineers. She believes in all things paranormal, a closet full of designer bags, weekly manicures, the Law of Attraction, aliens, angels, and the value of a graduate degree in psychology. Her debut audiobook, *Among Us* was featured on Audible's ACX University and is an Audible Editors Select pick.

Visit her online at
KristinaRienzi.com

ACKNOWLEDGMENTS

When I first wrote *Breaking Evil*, I was in an emotional fog. It was 2014 into 2015, the years my mom was diagnosed with cancer and then passed away. Being present in life wasn't easy for me back then, but pouring my emotions into a story sure helped.

I can't recall writing this book. It was as if *Breaking Evil* wrote itself. Through it all, what stands out for me most is that my mom was so proud of me, even when she was going through what would become the end of her life. So most importantly, I must acknowledge her, sending a prayer to Heaven to thank her for always being my biggest champion, my most loyal fan, and forever the person who loved me *more*. I will always pursue my passions in life because of the amazing woman who raised me to be my very best, even with all my flaws. She never got to see this book get published (originally back in 2016), but I believe she knows the gift writing has been to me in my life, especially during the hardest times, and is grateful. I'll miss her until we meet again.

On to 2018, when I got my rights back to the Ensouled

Series and subsequently sent *Breaking Evil* (and its prequel, *Choosing Evil*) into shiny new edits and publication.

There isn't enough gratitude in the world to thank the two men who are my closest family, supporting me through everything in life: my husband, Tom, and my dad. If it weren't for your support and ability to appreciate my introverted, writerly self while spending hours behind the laptop to create my fictional worlds, no books would be published. I love you both to the end of the universe and back!

I must also thank my incredible author assistant extraordinaire, Kate Tilton, of course! You make the publishing magic happen. I'm enamored by your drive—always pushing me to do what's right by the industry and my heart. You work tirelessly to make sure I meet my goals, and I'm truly grateful.

To my editor and friend, Christie Stratos...you rock, girl! Thank you so much for coming to the rescue for me. I'm so grateful you approached me at Belmar BookCon years ago with your camera and ball of energy. I'm so impressed by your passion and work ethic. You inspire me! Thank you for shining my stories into precious diamonds.

Readers, especially my Rienzi Rebels, these books are for you! You have my love, always.